BK F . B714B
BURMA RIFLES, A STORY OF MERRILLS MARAUD
1960 .00 FV
3000 125411 30015
St. Louis Community College
W9-DFW-621

# Burma Rifles

# Burma Rifles

A STORY OF MERRILL'S MARAUDERS

By Frank Bonham

THOMAS Y. CROWELL COMPANY · NEW YORK

*This book is dedicated to all those Americans of Japanese ancestry who served with the armed forces of the United States in World War II.*

*In particular it is the author's wish to commemorate the heroism of the fourteen Nisei volunteers with the 5307th Composite Unit (Provisional)—popularly known as "Merrill's Marauders"—whose very presence behind the enemy lines in Burma involved courage beyond the call of duty.*


*Manufactured in the United States of America by the Vail-Ballou Press, Inc., Binghamton, New York*
*Library of Congress Catalog Card No. 60-11535*
*Eighth Printing*

# FOREWORD

In the months following the attack by the Japanese on Pearl Harbor, thousands of Japanese-American residents of the Pacific Coast were hastily rounded up and herded into relocation centers. For the most part, these people lost their homes and property in this sudden move. In nearly all cases, they were deprived of their freedom for the duration of the war.

The nine relocation centers where they were interned for varying periods consisted of camps of tar-paper barracks located in the bleaker sections of the West and Midwest. They were cold in winter, hot in summer. The streets varied from muddy, to frozen, to dusty. Food was poor and housing inadequate.

Having made these Americans of Japanese ancestry as uncomfortable as possible, the Army then sent among them a recruiting team with the task of persuading young Niseis to volunteer for extra-hazardous duty.

It is a tribute to the character of the Japanese-American that thousands of Niseis responded. The achievements of the famous 442nd "Go for Broke" Infantry Regiment are well known. Less well known is the fact that another nearly six thousand Niseis served in the Pacific and China-Burma-India theaters of war as interpreters, translators, and intelligence and reconnaissance men with combat units.

During the past two years it has been my privilege to talk with many Niseis who served with the armed forces in World War II, as well as others who spent the war in relocation centers. To their credit it can be said that little bitterness remains over their treatment at the hands of their government in 1942. One of the laudable characteristics of the Japanese is a willingness to forget past unhappiness and live in the present. To know Japanese-Americans is to admire their forthrightness, industry, and resilience. These are qualities we like to think of as typically American—and that is what it seems to have taken an armed conflict to make us aware of: that the Japanese-American is basically no different from any other American.

I should like to express here my thanks to some of the persons who have aided me in the research involved in the writing of this book. Valuable assistance was given by many Niseis and Kibeis, of whom the following is only a partial list:

Sergeant Stanley Uno; Harry K. Andow; Soichi Fukui; Koichi Shibuya; Harry Akune; Sho Nomura; Cappy Harada; Ben Sugeta; Kenny Yasui; George Omatsu; and Sam Kawano.

Special thanks is due Sergeant Uno, an ex-Marauder himself and the first Japanese member of the Los Angeles Police Department to be made a sergeant of detectives, who started a train of thought one day by suggesting that someone should write the story of the Niseis with Merrill's Marauders.

Published material dealing specifically with the Marauders has been difficult to find. The most detailed history of the Marauders, and indeed an outstanding and thoughtful book by any standards, is Charlton Ogburn's, *The*

*Marauders.* An ex-Marauder also, Mr. Ogburn has achieved what will probably remain the definitive work on that tragic and heroic group. Other works of great value to me were the American Forces in Action Series publication, *Merrill's Marauders;* Charles F. Romanus and Riley Sunderland's *Stilwell's Command Problems;* and General Stilwell's own work, *The Stilwell Papers.*

General works on the CBI and the Burma campaign which were helpful were *Marsmen in Burma,* by J. H. Randolph; *Beyond the Chindwin,* by Bernard Fergusson; *Retreat with Stilwell,* by Jack Belden; *Grand Strategy,* by the British government printing office; *Burma Surgeon,* by Gordon S. Seagrave; and *Burma Surgeon Returns,* by the same author.

Other sources consulted were *Citizen 13,660,* by Miné Okuba; *Americans from Japan,* by Bradford Smith; and the *Military Intelligence Service Language School Album.*

But books can never impart the "I-was-there" sensation as graphically as word-of-mouth recollections of one who actually lived through an experience, and I wish to thank all those who took the time and trouble to provide me with what was invaluable assistance in this effort.

In the writing of this book, for story purposes it was necessary to telescope some of the events of the Second World War into a shorter time span than they actually occupied.

FRANK BONHAM

*Rancho Santa Fe, California*
*1960*

# CONTENTS

## CHAPTER 1

# Pearl Harbor

The fog had stolen in the night before, a long gray bank rolling in off the ocean. Like a blotter, it absorbed all shapes and sounds as it traveled inland. It was so dense that in Jerry's home they could scarcely hear the automobiles creeping along the highway before the farmhouse.

It was still heavy at dawn when he went out to work in the field with his father and younger brother. For two hours he chopped at the weeds that managed to thrive winter and summer in the mild Southern California climate. He saw the beads of dew sliding down the spears of the young plants to water the coarse earth, and his father said hopefully, "Another good fog tonight and we won't have to irrigate. Four nights of fog are as good as one day of rain."

Jerry was always skeptical of these old saws of his father's. To him they smacked of superstition. He had too logical and inquiring a mind to take such beliefs on faith. (How heavy a fog? How light a rain?) So he tested this particular saying with the rain gauge at school one winter. They had four good fogs in a row—but there was too little moisture in the gauge to measure. And if there was too little to measure, he reasoned, there was too little to water the earth.

But somehow the fog got into the ground; and from the ground it was siphoned up into the roots; and from the roots it traveled into the stems and leaves of the plants—and they did not have to irrigate. He decided there was some factor in the phenomenon which he had missed. So he had to accept this particular superstition as his father did—on faith.

Now, as he drove the pickup truck into Compton to buy the Sunday papers, the white sea mist was rising from the earth, leaving the soil black and moist, with farm buildings and fields mysteriously emerging from the grayness like a print developing in a photographer's tray. Just as he reached town, the whole sky began to brighten with a pearly luminosity, as though the world had been slipped inside a great pink sea shell. Somehow it gave Jerry a feeling that something exciting was about to happen.

After parking before the drugstore, he took two papers off the rack. He felt strong, full of energy, and happy—he wasn't sure why, except that he had the rest of the day to himself to clean up his homework and tinker with his transmitter.

As he entered the drugstore, he heard a radio voicing a news broadcast. A dozen men were grouped by the cigar counter, talking in hushed, excited voices. Jerry knew at once that something out of the ordinary was taking place; for more than three or four customers to gather in Clark's

Drugstore on a Sunday morning was exceptional. The men reminded him of the groups that clustered in stores during the world series to listen to the games. But in this case the radio was hardly audible over the strong buzz of conversation.

Then one of the men, Sid Shafer, noticed Jerry, and Jerry saw him touch the arm of another man; and this man, too, peered at him with a curious intensity. Then he murmured something to a man standing near him, and in a moment the drugstore was almost silent, while everyone looked at Jerry. He glanced behind him to see whether someone else was standing there. No one was.

Puzzled, he gazed at Mr. Clark, the druggist, who returned his gaze with the embarrassed expression of someone about to admit, "Well, well—we were just talking about you!"

Jerry smiled at him. "What's the matter?"

"Nothing, son," said Mr. Clark, unconvincingly. "Did you want to pay for those papers?"

Jerry approached the cash register. The druggist rang up the sale and returned Jerry's change. Men were beginning to murmur again, but still there was that slowed-down sense of things being out of gear. Jerry gave up and turned to leave. Then he saw that Sid Shafer had drifted near the door. Shafer, a real estate man, watched Jerry with lazy attention. He was a very tall, thin man with curly black hair and small blue eyes.

"Nice fog last night," Jerry said.

"Uh-huh," Shafer said.

"Maybe we won't have to irrigate this week. My father says four nights of fog are as good as one day of rain."

He did not particularly like Shafer, who had been trying for three years to persuade Jerry's father to sell their small farm, and seemed to take it personally that he did not care to.

"That what he says?" Shafer said, winking at someone. "Sounds like old-country hogwash to me."

"It used to to me. In fact, I checked it with a rain gauge. It didn't check out scientifically—but for some reason it seems to work!"

Some of the men chuckled. They knew Jerry was always exploring the scientific basis for some widely accepted notion, such as, "Curly hair becomes kinky in wet weather," or "Holding a match in the teeth while peeling onions will keep the eyes from watering."

"What else does your dad say?" asked Shafer, with his jeering smile.

Jerry was puzzled. "About what?"

"The war, for instance."

"What about the war?" Jerry was sure Shafer was trying to make a point, but he was not sure what the point was.

"Seems like a foxy character like your old man would have *something* to say about it. It's a pretty big thing, ain't it?"

Jerry shrugged. "He thinks we'll probably have to get into it, sooner or later. Why?"

"I was just thinking: you'll probably be the first kid from Junior College to enlist, won't you?"

Jerry felt the nettling of his temper. "Why should I?"

Mr. Clark said loudly, behind the cigar counter, "See you later, boy." Then he spoke quickly to another man, trying to get a conversation going about the price of oat hay. But as Jerry started past Shafer, the realtor tapped his arm.

"Maybe you ain't heard the news this morning, huh?"

"What news?"

Jerry became aware of something the radio was saying, and now Shafer tilted his head to signify "Listen—!"

". . . is reported to have been sunk with all hands. In addition, the battleships *West Virginia, Oklahoma,* and *Nevada* have been sunk. The attack on Pearl Harbor by Japan came while—"

Jerry was shocked. For over a year there had been tension between the United States and Japan, but no one in Jerry Harada's family had had any thought of its ending in a war. He could hardly comprehend that a little nation like Japan had actually attacked the most powerful country in the world. He gazed wordlessly around the group of men.

"What's he going to say about that, junior?" Shafer was demanding angrily. "Maybe he didn't know the attack was coming, huh? Not much! Every Jap on the Coast has been primed and waitin'!"

"Oh, let him alone, Sid," the druggist growled. "I don't think our Japanese knew a thing about it. Jerry's lived here all his life. He's as American as any other kid."

Jerry was suddenly conscious—more than he had ever been—of being Japanese himself. He glanced down at the papers he carried—a *Times* for himself and his sister and brother; a *Rafu Shimpo* for his parents, who read very little English. He had an impulse to slide the *Rafu Shimpo* out of sight under the other paper, but decided staunchly, Why should I? We're Americans, even if we do read Japanese. Is that a crime?

Shafer was saying breathlessly to the druggist, "He's American like sukiyaki! Bet there's a regular arsenal under the Haradas' greenhouse. And how about that radio transmitter of his? I always said we were fools to let the Japs own property this close to the coast! I tell you, we're sittin' on a powder keg!"

Jerry said stiffly, staring at him, "We didn't know anything about it. We've been out in the field since sunup."

Shafer grinned at the others. "How's a white man going to beat competition like that? The whole family out workin' at dawn on Sunday!"

"You can't beat it by hanging around the pool hall like some people," said Mr. Clark, and the other men laughed.

Jerry gazed urgently at him. "Is it really true—have they bombed Pearl Harbor?"

"Sure sounds like it, son," said the druggist.

Jerry turned and started out. He felt the way you feel after a blind-side tackle in a football game—shaken and confused. There was nothing anyone could do now but wait. There would be a family council at which Mr. Harada would discuss the awkward position the Japanese-Americans had been thrown into, and perhaps it would make more sense, then.

"Maybe some of us will drop around later," Shafer said mildly.

"What for?" Jerry demanded.

"Check around a little for guns and the like."

"You'd better come with a search warrant, if you do."

Shafer tapped his chest. "Now, don't randy with your betters, Michio—that's your name, ain't it? A lot of other folks are going to wonder about where you people stand in this. Better not give anyone the idea you stand with the Japs."

"Why should we? My parents have lived here for twenty years. I was born here. I've gone to American schools all my life, and most of my friends are Caucasians."

"Plus, you went to Japanese language school—and spent a year in Japan, didn't you?" Shafer reminded him.

"I went to language school Saturday afternoons—because my folks didn't want me to lose the language. And I stayed with an aunt and uncle in Japan to learn something about the country. But Russ Bennett went to language school too—does that make him disloyal?"

Russ was the son of an insurance broker in Compton. He and Jerry had been friends since first grade—had played together, studied together, built radio transmitters together. And because many of Mr. Bennett's clients were Japanese farmers and truckers, he had encouraged his son to learn the language, in case Russ should follow him in the business some day. His Japanese-American business was steadily growing, and the Japanese were always good pay. Russ had a good hold on Japanese through visiting with the Harada family; and because he enjoyed it, he had gone to language school with Jerry. He spoke nearly as fluent Japanese as Jerry himself.

Shafer was grinning as Jerry stared angrily at him. "Let's hear a little Japanese, Michio. Let's see what you learned in that language school."

Jerry looked him over, and said softly, "*Baka ni tsukeru kusuri nashi.*"

"Pretty good," Shafer commented. "What's it mean?"

" 'There is no medicine for stupidity,' " Jerry quoted. "It's another of those sayings of my father's."

CHAPTER 2

# The Proud Americans

One day, several years before, an airplane had crashed on the Harada farm only a hundred feet from the main building. It had taken off from a small airport two miles up the highway, had skimmed along above the power lines, and at last had sunk like a big, clumsy bird to the ground. The pilot, who had suffered a broken nose, returned the following day with a pair of black eyes and some adhesive tape striping his face, to supervise the removal of two ordinary automobile engines from the craft.

Then he presented himself at the Harada house. "Have you got any use for that junk out there?" he asked Mr. Harada, almost angrily.

"You mean the airplane?" Mr. Harada asked politely.

"If you could call it that. It was an experimental job. I've taken off everything I can use. If you want the rest of it you can have it. Maybe you can use it for a henhouse." The flier sounded utterly disgusted.

"Thank you very much," Mr. Harada smiled. "Perhaps we can use it for a hothouse for tropical plants. Thank you very much."

But it was never used for tropical plants; it became an

extra bedroom. When it was found that Jerry could almost stand up in the cabin of the oversized monoplane, and that there was room for a small cot, a chair, and a desk, it was decided that he could have it for his bedroom; his sister Helen would move into his old bedroom and Jerry's younger brother, who had shared the room with him, would move into the smaller bedroom Helen had occupied. (Helen's real name was Hanako, meaning "flower," but no one but her parents had called her that for years.)

Everybody won on this airplane transaction except the pilot-inventor, who was never seen again. Jerry had a bedroom with a tail-skid (the wheels had been removed), Helen had a large bedroom all her own, and Sam, the younger boy, had a small bedroom to himself.

As he drove back that morning, Jerry saw that his father was still working in the field among the spindly little junipers. Twelve-year-old Sam was in the lath-house tagging camellia and azalea plants. Obviously they had not heard the bad news. Jerry was glad. He had a strong desire to talk to Russ before he talked to anyone else.

After parking, he hurried down the path to XP9960, his bedroom. The path ran between lath-houses glowing with color—the shade plants having just come into bloom, barely in time for the Christmas trade. Out beyond the buildings were a rough corral and a small barn where the workhorses were kept. From the roof of the barn rose a high, whiplike tower from the tip of which an antenna swung like a spider web to another tower near Jerry's cabin.

It was necessary to stoop after entering the cabin, and Jerry crouched and went back to the rear of the room, which was crowded with racks of transformers, tubes, and coils. He snapped on the current and sat at the operator's desk. While the tubes warmed, he waited with his chin in his hands, thinking about the war and wondering how many people would react like Sid Shafer—regarding the Japanese-Americans as enemies.

The strong hum of the transmitter came up, and Jerry selected Russ's wave length. Sunday mornings, Russ usually worked with his own set. Before calling him, Jerry turned on his receiver and put on his headphones.

Almost at once he heard Russ's voice. ". . . Calling W6UC. Come on, W6 Utter Confusion—let's hear from you!"

Jerry realized he must have been calling for some time. He switched on the mike.

"W6UC calling W6EG. What's on your mind?"

Eight miles away, Russ said, "I've been calling you for the last hour. I didn't want to call you on the telephone if we could get together this way. I guess you've heard the news."

Jerry threw the switch over. "They must be crazy, Russ! How can they last six months against the United States?"

"I don't know, but I know one thing for sure: you and I will both be getting a call from the draft board pretty darned soon. They'll call up the reserves and R.O.T.C. first."

"They'll call you, maybe—I don't know about me," Jerry said uncertainly.

"Why not?"

"I'm a Nisei, you know—second-generation Japanese."

"What of it? You're an American citizen. Any citizen can bear arms in defense of his country, can't he?"

"I don't know. There's never been a situation just like this before. I was talking to Sid Shafer in the drugstore this morning—"

Russ's voice rasped in the headphones. "That pinhead! All he knows is property values! If a volcano blew up the heart of Los Angeles, the only thing he could talk about would be the effect on property values. The only 'situation' I know of is that you're nineteen years old, and an officer in R.O.T.C. And don't forget you speak Japanese! Believe me, they're going to be scratching for translators!"

Jerry felt encouraged. "I hadn't thought of that."

Japanese was not the kind of language you could learn in a year or two; ideas are not even expressed as they are in English, and the beautiful little symbols in which they are written, though intricate and graceful, are like so many puzzles to a person who does not have years of experience in reading them.

"Are you going to enlist?" Jerry asked.

"I don't know yet. I'll have to talk to my folks first. I

don't think we'll have to enlist anyway—they'll probably be inviting us in before we have time!"

Jerry left the shack and went toward the house to tell his parents the bad news. But as he was walking toward it, he saw his mother hurrying down the aisles of tiny juniper trees toward his father in the field. Mr. Harada straightened up and watched her come. And now he began walking slowly toward her, and Jerry thought, He's guessed. . . .

In the house, he found his sister Helen gazing out the window at her parents. The radio was giving another of the incessant news reports. Helen was a pretty girl with very large eyes for an Oriental, and a long page-boy bob exactly like the ones all the girls at high school were wearing. She was sixteen. Helen was wearing a little lipstick these days, after a long campaign with her mother. And as she looked at Jerry she suddenly bit her lower lip and her eyes filled with tears.

"Did—did you hear—?" she started to ask him.

Jerry put his arm around her shoulders. "It'll be okay, sis. The war can't last long."

Helen put a handkerchief to her nose and controlled her weeping. "But can we still go to school?"

"Why not?" Jerry laughed. "We haven't flunked out just because there's a war on! And we're not enemy aliens, are we?"

"I—I don't know. I hope not."

Sam, their younger brother, came into the house. He was still carrying a handful of little wooden plant tags like tongue depressors. He looked at Jerry and Helen, puzzled by their silence.

"What's the matter with everybody?" he asked. "I just saw Mom going out in the field bawling. Hey—you've been bawling too!" he accused his sister.

"Oh, shut up!" Helen said through the handkerchief. She could barely endure her younger brother sometimes. The heaviest cross she had to bear was that, in old-country fashion, the women of the family bathed last, so that she had to have her bath in the same water her dirty little brother had washed in. (Actually, everyone always washed first in a small tub before getting into the big zinc-bottomed wooden water barrel with the fire burning under it.)

"What's the matter with her?" Sam asked Jerry.

"The Japanese have bombed Pearl Harbor," Jerry said grimly.

Sam scratched his short black hair with a plant tag. "What's Pearl Harbor?"

"It's a big naval base in Hawaii. You ought to know that—you've studied geography."

"Oh, yeah. . . . What do you mean, they've *bombed* it!" he asked.

"Oh, go look it up!" Helen told him loftily. She went into her bedroom and slammed the door.

Sam grinned at Jerry. "Boy, is she wound up!"

"Look, sprout—we're in this deal up to our ears," Jerry

told him soberly. "We're at war with Japan, now. We'll have to fight just like the English are doing. We'll probably get into the fight with Germany, too."

"Gosh," Sam said. "Will—will you have to go in the army?"

"Maybe. If they'll take me," Jerry added.

In the rear, the kitchen door screeched open. Their mother and father could be heard wiping their shoes on the mat. Then they came into the living room, Mrs. Harada clenching her hands together and looking down. Jerry's father was sober and tense.

"Please tell Hanako to come," Mr. Harada told Jerry.

Helen had been listening, for she reappeared from her room at once, and walked with her eyes lowered to a chair where she sat down to wait in silence. Mrs. Harada sat down also, and Sam moved toward a chair. Family councils were serious matters in the Japanese home. Jerry hesitated and then took a chair.

"Your mother has just heard over the radio that we are at war with Nippon," said Mr. Harada formally, in Japanese. "We will pray that it ends quickly in victory for our beloved country. In the meantime, we must consider how to conduct ourselves. . . ."

He paused, and Jerry nerved himself for what was ahead—exhortations to calmness and humility.

"Do you all know of the cherry trees which bloom around the Washington monument in our nation's capital?"

asked Mr. Harada. He did not wait for their replies, but went on, standing there small and muscular and brown, massaging his hands together.

"The trees were presented to the United States by the government of Japan, long ago. Every spring they burst into glorious bloom, so heavy with cherry blossoms that their white petals drift like snow. Those trees came as mere whips from Nippon. One might say they were born in the Orient —but it was the soil of America which nourished them."

He gave each of the children a solemn gaze.

"And so it is with you. All of you are descendants of Japanese ancestors—but it is America which has given you strength and health, and the opportunity to become more than field laborers or pullers of rickshaws. You have a great debt to your country."

Jerry felt his mother's eyes on him as she smiled proudly at him.

"We must be sure," continued Mr. Harada carefully, "that our neighbors realize we appreciate what America has done for us. We must show it by our humility—by our readiness to do what is asked of us."

"What will they ask us to do, Pop?" asked Sam.

"Who can say? But if anyone doubts our loyalty, we will be quick to prove it. And we must be very careful—"

"Careful about what?" Jerry asked.

"Not to offend anyone who challenges us."

"But we're not guilty of anything!" protested Jerry. "Our neighbors owe as much to America as we do."

"No—because we came as guests. We must be good guests, therefore. . . ."

Jerry looked down, frowning at his hands. That's all right for you, he thought. You were born in Japan—you learned humility before you learned to walk. But we're Niseis—born here—and we've been taught to be proud, not humble. I'm proud of being an American, and I want to act like it. And if people like Sid Shafer try to make out that I'm anything but a proud American, I'll show them where they're wrong. . . .

"Do you all understand?" asked his father.

"Yes, Father," murmured Helen.

"Uh-huh," said Sam confusedly.

"Michio," Mr. Harada said to Jerry.

"I don't understand why we should be humble," Jerry said. "We've been taught to be proud of being Americans."

"But others may mistake our pride for defiance!"

"What if somebody like Sid Shafer tries to tell people we're spies?"

"Spies?" His father frowned.

"This morning when I bought the papers he was in the drugstore with a lot of other men. Shafer told me he might come out to see if we had a lot of guns and ammunition buried under the house. What do we do if he comes?"

For the first time, Mrs. Harada spoke, rubbing her hands slowly together and speaking anxiously. "Your father and I came to this country with only a few dollars—without even the language. But we were young and willing to work.

We worked in the fields like slaves until we had saved enough to buy our land. In Nippon we could never have owned land. But here we have land, a home, children who already have more education than we. But we have more experience than they; and we know how much may be lost by not being careful—"

"But you can lose by being too careful, Mom!"

Smiling faintly, Mr. Harada said, "It will never happen to you, my son. Being careful has never been your trouble. Perhaps that is because you were born in the Year of the Tiger. Sons of the Tiger are always rash."

"Then there must be a lot of rash Niseis around. Most of the kids in my class are the same age I am."

"I was born in the Year of the Horse, wasn't I, Pop?" Sam asked.

"Yes," Helen said. "Strong and stupid."

Sam turned on her. "Who's talking? I'll bet you were born in the Year of the Top—dizzy!"

"Children!" Mrs. Harada reproved. "Every year is a good year, if we make it one. But it is up to all of you to be—careful, for a while."

## CHAPTER 3

# "Run Them Out!"

But during the next few weeks it became clear that being careful would make no difference whatever in what happened to the Japanese on the Pacific Coast.

Only a few people went out of their way to be unfriendly to Jerry's family and the thousands of other Japanese-Americans living in the Los Angeles area. But one day Jerry saw a card in a barbershop reading: *Japs Shaved: Not Responsible for Accidents.* And a small restaurant advertised: *This restaurant poisons both rats and Japs.* But the barbershop was a small and dirty one, and the restaurant was one which had the reputation of poisoning everyone without discrimination.

Most people tried to behave as though nothing had happened. At worst, they were self-conscious in the presence of the Niseis. Jerry's friends at school were still his friends. Yet somehow a feeling of ill will began to close suffocatingly about all the Japanese up and down the Pacific Coast. Most of it seemed to have its origin in newspaper editorials. "A Jap's a Jap," and "112,000 Potential Enemies!" were two that Jerry read with anger.

One evening there was a hard rapping on the door.

Jerry opened it and saw Sid Shafer standing under the porch light. He was grinning as he slapped his palm with a folded newspaper. "Howdy, son," he said. "Folks here?"

"What do you want?" Jerry asked. He heard his father's footsteps crossing the room.

"Yes?" Mr. Harada said, stopping behind Jerry.

Shafer flapped the newspaper casually. "I thought maybe you hadn't heard the news. They're running the slope-heads out."

"Slope-heads?" repeated Mr. Harada.

"Buddha-heads—Japs!" Shafer smiled. "Kinda tough on you people, I guess, but that's what the papers are saying."

Jerry took the paper from his hand and glanced at the headline: ALL JAPANESE TO BE MOVED FROM WEST COAST AREAS! He handed the paper back to Shafer. For a moment he was too stunned to know how to answer. All his life he had lived here, most of it on this small farm. He had no idea where they would go if they left. He felt a little squeeze of homesickness for everything he had loved about his life.

Shafer glanced curiously about the living room as though he were appraising it. "Guess you know how much your farm will be worth once this news gets spread around. If you haven't sold by the time you have to move, you'll just about have to give it away. . . . What do you say to thirteen hundred for the whole layout?" he asked suddenly.

"No," Mr. Harada replied firmly, shaking his head. But he remained friendly in his manner toward the realtor.

"I won't haggle with you over some worn-out goat pasture," Shafer said. "I'll go fifteen hundred, but that's it. What do you say?"

"He said *no,*" Jerry told him. "You've been trying to get this 'goat pasture' for three years. If we have to sell, it won't be to you."

Shafer moved up suddenly and seized Jerry by the shoulder, his small blue eyes cold and venomous. His thumb dug painfully into Jerry's shoulder muscle.

"Going to give you some advice, junior—don't get smart with a white man *this* year. So you were captain of a ball team—that's great, but it ain't worth much now. And when I say something to you, you'd better—"

His hand gave Jerry's shoulder a twist—and Jerry's temper snapped. He stepped out and seized a handful of Shafer's shirt, slipped his foot past Shafer's, and gave him a quick pull to the side. It was a simple judo throw most of the boys at school knew. Shafer caught his breath and grabbed desperately at Jerry to retain his balance. But it was too late, and he flipped over on his side and fell flat from two feet off the cement floor. He rolled over on his back with a groan.

For a moment Jerry was afraid he had injured him. The realtor lay there blinking up at him with a deep, painful frown in his eyes. Behind Jerry, Mr. Harada exclaimed angrily and tried to pull Jerry inside. Jerry was filled with rage for the cruel stupidity of this man who had come to frighten some helpless people into sacrificing everything they had slaved for for twenty years.

Gradually, Shafer's eyes cleared, and then filled with fury. He scrambled up and went after Jerry with a long, looping blow at his head. Jerry ducked under the swing and locked a quick strangle hold on Shafer—his wrists crossed so that he was gripping the yoke of the man's shirt on opposite sides of his neck. The edge of his right wrist was locked hard against Shafer's windpipe, and the harder he pulled on the shirt the more impossible it was for Shafer to relieve the pressure that was choking him. Shafer struggled, hitting wildly at Jerry's face, but Jerry kept his head buried between his shoulders and choked the big man until finally he sagged to his knees. Then he stepped back.

Jerry's father pulled him back into the room as Shafer got up dazedly, massaging his throat. "You could kill a man that way!" he gasped.

"Yes, and you could have broken my shoulder, if you'd known how."

"I warned you!" Shafer panted. "Don't say I didn't warn you."

Jerry let his father pull him into the house. He slumped onto the sofa, as Shafer spoke furiously to his father. "You Japs think you can claim land just like you were citizens. Well, you aren't—and you never will be!"

"I—I try to become a citizen!" Mr. Harada protested.

"I try to pass tests—I know about George Washington and the Constitution, but—I can't express—"

"You want to have the cream and pour the skimmed milk down our throats! Well, mister, maybe we got something to say about that too—"

"We don't claim anything, Mr. Shafer. We love this country; we try to be good members of the community. Please forgive my son. He is young, the blood is hot. I will instruct him."

"Yeah—instruct him for me, too!" Shafer walked stiffly down the path to the driveway.

In the silent living room, Jerry looked at his father. Mr. Harada loomed above him angrily, his lips pressed to a thin line. Sam's voice came through the angry tension.

"Boy, you sure told him, Jerry!"

"Go to your room," Mr. Harada said furiously.

Jerry felt tears of frustration coming to his eyes. "Don't you understand how I feel? Just because we're Japanese, we don't have to take insults from him."

"An insult from a stupid man is nothing—nothing." Mr. Harada shook his head impatiently. "When your mother and I first came to this country, we were ridiculed and threatened. But what would have happened if my friends and I had broken store windows and fought with our tormentors? Would we be living in America today?"

Jerry knew his father was right. But that was different; his parents were not citizens, but he and Helen and Sam were. Wasn't it as wrong for Shafer to try to take advantage of Niseis, now, as it would be for him to bait Russ Bennett's family?

Confused and resentful, he left the house and shut himself in his bedroom. He tried to think about his studies, but all he could think about was what the paper had said —that all West Coast Japanese were to be evacuated to inland areas. What did that mean? To concentration camps, as in Germany?

He put his books away and turned on the radio to get the news. The commentator was pronouncing in a deep, voice-of-doom tone:

". . . Meantime it has been reported that flashlight signals have again been sighted in the Japanese community above San Pedro. From this point, high above the sea, signals can be sighted by Japanese submarines or warships off our coast. I was talking to an officer in General De Witt's headquarters today and learned that a deadline will be set shortly after which all Japanese remaining on the Pacific Coast will be forcibly evacuated to other locations. . . ."

Jerry snapped it off in disgust.

Do people really believe that stuff? he wondered. The rumors sounded as though they had come straight out of cloak-and-dagger mystery stories. Tales of tuna boats with machine guns hidden in the bait tanks . . . fishermen photographing the coastline and charting all the coves and harbors—although such charts were for sale in many bookstores and all boat supply houses. Arsenals under Japanese homes and powerful transmitters in attics! Had it not been cruel to the people about whom the stories were told, it would have been funny.

But Jerry realized something, finally. People were scared. They really feared the Coast might be invaded, and they had to have someone to vent their fear on. Manila had been lost to the Japanese; Midway and Wake Islands had fallen; people expected the Hawaiian Islands to be invaded any day. After that the next jump would be the Pacific Coast.

Jerry tried to get Russ on the radio, but there was no response to his call. Disappointed, he went back to his homework and put in a couple of hours on a term paper. Yet it seemed pointless. If they were to be evacuated, why work for grades that would not count? He shoved the books away—and stopped still, listening. A car had swung quietly into the drive.

Jerry went to the door and looked out, hoping to see Russ's Model A draw up before the garage. A car coasted in gently and stopped, its lights off. Jerry did not recognize it, and he was puzzled that the lights should have been turned off. Then three doors slammed in quick succession, and footfalls approached the old vine-grown airplane. A cramp of anxiety caught at Jerry. He jumped down and watched the men who were approaching—three men who came purposefully up the path between the lath-houses. Fear hit him a quick, numbing blow when he saw that each of them carried a weapon of some kind.

They stopped in the fall of light from a window and stared grimly at him. One of the men was Sid Shafer. He, like the others, carried a baseball bat so new the varnish gleamed.

"Stay out of the way and you won't get hurt," he warned.

"What's the idea?" Jerry demanded.

"Suppose you just listen for a change. You've got a radio transmitter in there, haven't you?"

Jerry gazed at the men with him; they looked shabby and somehow uneasy. "Yes, and I've got a license to operate it," he said.

"Oh, no. Not tonight, you haven't. Maybe you ought to listen to the news instead of talking to Japanese gunboats. All ham outfits have been ordered shut down."

"They haven't notified me."

"That's what we're here for," one of the men chuckled. He shook the baseball bat he carried. "This here is your notice."

Shafer walked forward and peered into the cabin. "Pretty snug, boys. Regular command post." Jerry seized his arm as he started inside.

"If you meddle in there I'll call the police!"

He caught a movement from one of the other men as Shafer himself pulled away and raised the bat he carried. Jerry ducked and crouched against the plane with his arm raised to ward off the blow. Shafer chuckled and lowered the bat.

"That's a good kid. I won't touch any of your junk but the radio, so relax and behave yourself."

Shafer ducked inside, while the other men held Jerry at bay. He stood there, his mouth dry with anger, hearing the man move about the little bedroom. There was a scraping noise as a chair was pulled aside. Finally Shafer called, "Here goes nothing, boys!"

A bright jangle of glass startled Jerry; one of the men jumped, too. Jerry's heart convulsed. He recalled all the days of hard work, earning money to build the transmitter; he thought of the weeks of soldering, testing, regrouping components. Another splintering crash came from the cabin, and then a tinkling rainfall of glass.

There was a spray of light from the road. Headlights swung into the driveway, throwing slats of light through the lath-houses over the fuselage of the airplane. Both men averted their faces as the light briefly illuminated them. Up the drive came the grind of tires in gravel. But an instant later Jerry's heart sank as he heard them retreating. Then he realized that whoever had driven in was merely backing out so that his car would not block the driveway.

"Sid!" called one of the men. "Somebody comin'."

Shafer hunched into the door and looked out. "Who is it—cops?"

"Don't know. Just somebody that drove in and backed out again. But I reckon they're parking."

Shafer jumped down. He glanced at the bat he carried,

scarred now from hacking at the transmitter. He laid it back over his shoulder.

"You'd better not report this, unless you want more of the same," he warned Jerry.

"Let 'im report it!" another man shrugged. "It's his word against the word of citizens, ain't it?"

"Citizens!" Jerry said bitterly.

The men walked hurriedly back to their car and got into it. A moment later it turned around in the yard and went skidding back through the gravel to the highway.

## CHAPTER 4

# One Suitcase

Jerry climbed into the plane and gazed at the tangle of wires and broken glass Shafer had made of the transmitter. He wanted to weep; he wanted to fight back. A great pressure of rage and desperation built up in him. He could call the police, but he was not sure how much good it would do.

While he was going through the gleaming ruin of the radio, he heard someone else stop outside XP9960 and rap on the door.

"Come in," Jerry said dully.

Crawling was almost the only way Russ Bennett could get into the plane; he was six feet three inches tall. "If that boy ever gets his growth," Coach Wilson said once, "the telephone company will hang wires on him." He ducked into the cabin and squatted down by Jerry's cot.

"What's the matter? You look sadder than a kennel full of bloodhounds."

Jerry gestured at the wreckage. "Look!"

Russ stared. Then he walked back and sat in the operator's chair and gazed at the transmitter. "For Lord's sake, Jerry, what happened?"

"Sid Shafer and a couple of his pool-hall buddies came here tonight. They all had baseball bats. Shafer smashed my transmitter while the others kept me from stopping him."

Russ picked up a broken power tube. "You're kidding!"

"No, I'm not. I had a run-in with Shafer earlier this evening. He came back to get even, I guess."

"Have you called the police?"

"Not yet. Shafer just left."

"Then that's the car I saw leaving as I drove up. You're going to call the police, aren't you?"

"If Dad will let me. . . ."

"Why shouldn't he?"

"He's got a lot of funny ideas. You think he's just like anybody else, and then he comes up with some crazy idea about smiling and turning the other cheek."

Russ squeezed his arm. "I know how you feel, Jerry. I don't blame you for being sore. But I know how they feel, too. People have been half-afraid of Japanese and Chinese people ever since they first started coming to this country—the inscrutable Oriental, you know. Weird stories about the Chinese eating rat stew and the Japanese all being black-belt judo killers!"

It provoked a bitter chuckle from Jerry. "I know."

"All this is part of the same thing. They've never really known you, so they don't know what you're thinking now. They don't know where your loyalty is, really."

"If they don't, it's their own fault. They haven't made it easy for us to mingle with them—at least for the older people."

"Well—that's partly the language barrier. Don't think I approve of this attitude; I'm just trying to tell you why I think they're making such a fuss right now. People like Shafer—you'll find them everywhere, but they don't represent a very large part of the population."

Jerry knew it was all true. But it rankled, just the same. "Shafer said all ham licenses have been revoked. Have you heard anything about it?" Jerry asked.

"That's one reason I came over tonight. I had a special delivery letter about it. We're off the air as of now. The other reason I came is—I'm going in the army tomorrow!"

"No kidding!" Jerry stared quickly at him. He felt a stab of loneliness—loneliness for the good times they had had; for the beach; for after-school practice; for studies and vacations. For now it was over, and over so quickly and so sadly.

Russ pulled an envelope from his shirt pocket. " 'Greetings,' it says. I've been expecting it for a week."

"Did you enlist?" Jerry asked—hoping he had not, because it would mean he had kept it secret from him.

Russ looked down at the envelope, seeming embarrassed. "No—not exactly. I wish I could tell you more about it. It's—well, a special outfit I'm going to. I'll tell you about it as soon as I can."

"You do that," Jerry said dryly.

Russ punched his shoulder. "Aw, look—if it was anybody but Uncle Sam, I'd tell you right now. In fact—"

Jerry caught an edge of excitement in his voice which sent a tingle through him. "In fact, what? Is it a language school or something?"

For an instant Russ's guard was down, and his jaw sagged. He gazed blankly at Jerry, and Jerry knew he had hit it: Russ was going to a language school, or something similar. It was all so natural—a Caucasian like Russ speaking Japanese would be of tremendous value to the Army—that he was surprised he had not guessed it immediately. Russ looked aside, however.

"Old Big-mouth Bennett," he said. "Well, I don't have much time, kid—got to pack. I catch the big red car in the morning for the induction center." He put out his hand. "So I guess—"

Jerry's throat tightened as they shook hands. "It doesn't seem right," he said. "You going into the army—me staying behind. We've done so many things together that it's hard to get used to the idea. . . ."

Russ's hand squeezed hard. "Maybe you'll be in the army too, before you know it. I wouldn't be a bit surprised."

They went to the house, where Russ said good-bye to Jerry's family. Then he drove off. Jerry returned disconsolately to the plane. Although it did not seem to matter any more, he set about making a list of all the radio parts Sid Shafer had broken.

But the incident was never reported.

In the morning an olive-green sedan stopped before the house and two military policemen came to the door to speak to Mr. Harada. One of them gave him a paper printed in English and Japanese which announced that all Japanese were being relocated next week. Camps had been prepared for them in areas away from the Coast. A truck would come for them within a week. Each member of the family would be allowed one suitcase.

It was hard for any of them to believe it was really going to happen. But people had somehow been convinced by all the newspaper propaganda that the Japanese-Americans were just waiting for some signal to blow up bridges and buildings.

There was no time to get a fair price for the farm, the acres of seedlings in the field, nor for the hundreds of shade plants in the lath-houses. A man who owned a big Los Angeles newspaper came by one day and offered ten cents a plant for the camellias and azaleas. He was setting out thousands of shade plants on his estate. The camellias were worth a dollar each, but Mr. Harada accepted the offer rather than let the plants die.

The night before the truck was to come, each member of the family had his suitcase packed, and everything they had been unable to dispose of had been stored in the community church. The Haradas sat down to their last dinner in their home; but Jerry could not eat. He felt a coldness in his body like a bowl of cracked ice in his stomach. He heard Helen ask their mother fearfully, "Will it be like a jail, mother?"

Mrs. Harada smiled wearily. "Oh, I don't think so, Hanako."

"Well, will we have things like—well, school and—"

"—boy friends?" grinned Sam.

"All the important things, I'm sure," Mrs. Harada said.

"They're important, to Helen," Sam said.

"Oh, shut up," Helen said. But then she wrinkled her nose at him, and smiled. They began to eat.

In the morning an Army truck stopped before the house. It had a brown canvas top, with benches arranged along either side under the canvas. A number of other Japanese were already in the truck, small, silent people sitting with their suitcases on the floor. The Haradas carried their suitcases across the lawn, took their places inside the truck, and the engine roared into life.

Jerry gazed out the back as they rolled down the long driveway, swung east up the highway, and passed through Compton toward the distant mountains. In a short time the familiar landscape of farms and buildings was lost from sight. As surely as he knew anything, he knew they would never see them again.

# CHAPTER 5

# Topaz

At night, searchlights blazed along the barbed-wire fences enclosing the big camp of seven thousand Japanese evacuees. There were guard towers along the fence where soldiers with machine guns watched for persons trying to leave the camp. The blocks of long, dark barracks looked bleak under the star-shot Utah sky.

At first light, Jerry would hear the roosters beginning to crow. All about the camp they would send up their cheerful cries, and soon pans would begin to rattle in the mess halls. In the barracks of the Topaz Relocation Center, people would dress in the high-country cold and trudge down the streets to the wash-houses, carrying towels and toothbrushes.

The Japanese had all come at once, like an invasion of grasshoppers. Now it was early July, the summer heat had already begun, and up and down the dirt streets the dust blew in miniature cyclones. Each night it settled like dew; each morning the trucks and trampling feet would stir it up again.

After breakfast, bells would jangle and Sam and Helen and the other children would assemble in their classrooms.

All over camp the serious business of daily life would begin. In the Administration Building, young Nisei block administrators would make suggestions and present complaints, just like city councilmen. A few men who had been given jobs to relieve the critical work shortage in Topaz would leave by bus for the beet fields near the town. And Jerry would go to work in the camp laundry, where he folded sheets.

The thing which he and all the other Niseis commented on was that there were so many Japanese around. Like Jerry, most of the young people came from communities were they had lived among Caucasians, and now it was curious to see practically nothing but Oriental faces.

Camp life was a strange new way of living to them all. Every day there was a new, unsettling rumor, such as:

All Japanese were to be shipped back to Japan in exchange for American prisoners.

The Japanese would be kept penned up in centers forever, like Indians on reservations.

The food allotment was being cut.

The food allotment was being raised.

The camp was being moved to Alaska.

One noon there was a notice on the bulletin board at the Administration Building: *Volunteers for Army language school will be interviewed at 1400 hours today.*

Jerry ran all the way back to the barracks where he and his family lived in two bleak rooms. His mother was straightening up the rooms, though she had already straightened them up twice this morning. Internment had made her slow-moving and unhappy, for the things she loved to do—cook for her family, keep the home clean and bright—these things were impossible in a camp.

"What is it?" she asked quickly, as Jerry ran in.

"I'm trying out for language school!" Jerry exclaimed. "Where's my suit?"

Mrs. Harada brought it from a tall cardboard wardrobe. "It smells of mothballs," she said sadly.

"We'll all smell of mothballs," Jerry replied with a grin. There was such a warm fountain of excitement in him that he did not notice, at first, that his mother was on the point of weeping.

"Hey, what's wrong?" he asked, putting his arm around her. "This is just a tryout, like for a play. I'm not going to war tomorrow."

"But soon," she murmured. "Isn't that why they want you?"

"They need us, Mom," Jerry said earnestly. "There aren't many Americans who speak Japanese, but there are millions of Japanese who speak English. They need us for translators and interpreters."

"I know," she said humbly. "And I am glad to give my son to our country. Only I hope they will remember where they got him—and bring him back to me. . . ."

Jerry showered, dressed, shined his shoes, and at fourteen hundred hours—two o'clock—he was sitting in a waiting room among twenty other young Niseis. Rumors were whispered concerning the kind of duty which was going to be offered them—combat in the South Pacific—in Alaska—high-level translation work in Washington, D.C.

A door opened and a square-shouldered Nisei in uniform stepped into the room. Everyone stood quickly, but he smiled. "At ease," he said. "You're not in the Army yet." He wore a staff sergeant's chevrons and a shoulder patch Jerry did not recognize. It resembled a gopher's head. "I'm Sergeant Nomura. Is there anyone here who doesn't speak Japanese fluently?"

No one in the room admitted it if he did not.

"Good."

Sergeant Nomura went back into the room and the door remained closed for twenty minutes. It was Jerry's first experience with the mysterious ways of the Army. After a long time, the door opened again and the sergeant stepped back into the room and looked the men over.

"*Ki o tsuke!*" he said, in rapid Japanese.

For a moment it did not register with Jerry. Then he remembered the command from boyhood games: "Attention!" He stood quickly and brought his hands to his sides. Some of the others also obeyed the command, but most of the young men sat there, puzzled, and finally rose uncertainly, looking at one another.

"Boy, what a bunch of linguists you are!" the sergeant remarked. "*Ki o tsuke!* means 'Attention!' Okay, I want you to meet the man who will interview you—Lieutenant Bennett."

An officer came into the room behind him and looked them over. He was tall and slender in a crisply pressed uniform with new brass bars on the shoulders. It was Russ—Russ, looking tanned and much thinner, and very military. Jerry grinned, but Russ's eyes seemed to avoid him as he looked over the roomful of young Niseis.

"*Kon-nichi wa!*" he said.

"*Kon-nichi wa!*" they echoed.

"*Dozo o-kake kudasai.*"

On the command, they all sat down immediately. Russ glanced at a paper in his hand. "I suppose most of you have already figured out that the Army's in trouble for interpreters. They're needed for combat units as well as at fixed installations. Captured letters, maps, and battle orders are being thrown away unread because we haven't the men to translate them. Important prisoners are not being interrogated because there is no one to question them. To meet this need, the Army has opened a language school.

"The present course of study requires six months to complete. It includes, among other things, Japanese military language, history, and training in how to interrogate prisoners. The course isn't easy—it will be the equivalent of two years of college in six months."

He glanced at the wall clock. "Sergeant Nomura and I will be here today and this evening interviewing candidates for the school. We have ten relocation centers to cover in a few days, so each interview will have to be short."

At the last instant, his gaze came to Jerry and he winked. "Alphabetically, Sergeant," he murmured, and went back into the office.

As he awaited his turn, Jerry felt his bitterness toward the camp and the whole, brutal evacuation procedure beginning to fade into the back of his mind. To have something worth-while to do—to keep busy—that was the important thing. What ate away a man's morale like acid was idleness and uncertainty. And it came to him that the Niseis who were selected for Army service would occupy a very important position, for they would stand on high ground from which the whole country could view their every act. What these men did would help greatly to shape the nation's opinion of the Nisei population as a whole. It was a privilege and a responsibility.

When his turn came, he entered the room and closed the door. Russ came around the desk to shake hands with him. They smiled and looked each other over.

"What is this—coincidence?" Jerry asked.

"Not exactly. Sergeant Nomura and I are covering all of the relocation centers."

"You've sure lost that R.O.T.C. look!" Jerry chuckled. "You look old-Army now."

"I don't feel it. I'm green as grass. I just had three months of crawling under barbed wire at Fort Benning, and now I'm supposed to qualify as an infantry officer. I'd hate to take a platoon into battle tomorrow, I'll tell you."

Jerry smiled. "Where do you go next?"

"The same place you go! I can't tell you where—the Army's full of mysteries, you know—but we'll work as we've never worked before. Jaysee will seem like a vacation."

"Anything will seem better than camp life," Jerry said.

Russ nodded soberly. "I know. There's talk that they'll be placing the people from the camps on farms soon, so it should be better before long. In the meantime, all of you boys who pass the physical will take off for language school this week. The ones who come through with the best grades will be asked to volunteer for I. & R. duty overseas."

"What's that?"

"Intelligence and reconnaissance—hunting out the enemy and learning his strength. Combat, in other words."

A feeling of excitement ran like a cold finger down Jerry's spine. He knew the risks would be much greater for a Nisei than for an ordinary GI, since capture would almost surely mean torture. Yet the very danger brought a special thrill of its own. Russ seemed to know what he was thinking, for he said gravely:

"I don't have to tell you what you're getting into if you're accepted for I. & R. work. It'll be somewhere in the Pacific, of course, and a lot of it will be right up front. A battle order two days old isn't much help to the infantry—these documents have to be translated right now, and the sooner a prisoner can be questioned, of course, the better."

"I know what I'm getting into," Jerry said. "But I

figure somebody's got to do it, and it'll be worth the risks."

"Every Nisei I've talked to says the same thing," Russ said nodding. "I wish some of these newspaper publishers who've been running editorials on the sneaky Japs could follow me around for about one day. . . . Well, that's it," he said briskly. "If everything goes right, I'll see you in camp."

The following day was taken up with physical examinations and a series of written questionnaires. Only one of the twenty-two men who volunteered for ATIS, as the sergeant called it—Allied Translation and Interrogation Service—was turned down for physical reasons. The others were told to pack and wait.

That night, to Jerry's surprise, there was a farewell party for him in their rooms after dinner.

Somehow, Mrs. Harada had managed to get hold of a small white cake with the graceful Japanese character for *happiness* written on it in red icing. Mrs. Harada cut five small pieces of cake, with a double-sized piece for Jerry, who took a big bite and murmured with appreciation.

"How did you ever get this out of the cook?" he asked.

Everyone looked at Helen. "Helen got it out of her boy friend!" Sam reported with a laugh.

Helen gazed at him languidly. "He isn't my 'boy friend,' infant. He's just one of the guards. He likes to do things for us," she told Jerry. "So I asked him to try to buy a cake for us in town."

Mr. Harada produced something wrapped in tissue

paper. With a little bow, he presented it to Jerry. "Christmas in July?" Jerry smiled. He unwrapped the gift. It was a miniature camera of Japanese make. Touched, he looked up. "Where did you ever find a camera?"

"It was Mr. Miyano's," his mother told him. "We hope you will take pictures of your friends wherever you go, and have them take pictures of you."

"Sure, I will," Jerry said, examining the camera with appreciation.

"Now we speak of serious things," Mr. Harada said quietly. "In the Bible there is a passage which reads, 'You are the light of the world. A city which is set on a hill cannot be hid . . .' Nor can a man doing a job such as yours hide himself from the world. Whatever you do will be noticed. You will be fighting not only for your country; you will be fighting to prove the loyalty of us all."

"I know, Dad," Jerry said quietly. "Ever since I got this chance I've felt differently. Now I want to prove that the only thing different about us is our eyes and skin. . . ."

In the street there was a squeak of brakes. They all glanced toward the door, and Jerry's heart gave a thud. A knock came, and Mr. Harada opened it. A sergeant glanced into the lighted room. Jerry stood up quickly.

"Sorry to bother you folks. I'm looking for Michio Harada."

"That's me."

"Are you ready to travel?"

"All ready."

"Let's go," the sergeant said.

Mrs. Harada and Helen wept, Mr. Harada squeezed Jerry's hand and murmured, "*Sayonara!*" and Sam bashfully stood back waiting to be noticed. Jerry gave him a hug and said, "I'll bring you back an Arisaka rifle, Sammy."

He carried his suitcase outside, feeling chilly and hollowed-out, and climbed into the back of the truck.

## CHAPTER 6

# Savage

Nothing is so exciting, nor so bewildering, as arriving in a strange place at night. Your directions are confused; the air itself feels different; the darkness is full of unfamiliar sounds.

After three days on the train—most of the time being spent on sidings while other trains passed—the Topaz recruits reached a wooded area somewhere far northeast of Utah. Jerry was asleep on the hard plush seat when the train came to a halt after a series of lurches. Opening his eyes, he heard the ancient coach making sounds like an old man relaxing—its wooden bones creaking, steampipes sighing; and from directly under his feet came a clicking of cooling metal. He looked out and saw a lonely, steep-roofed station set against the blackness. He closed his eyes again and wearily tilted his head back; but at that moment someone mounted the steps of the car briskly.

A soldier came into the dim interior and looked at the Japanese faces sleepily gazing at him. "All right, you guys!" he announced. "This is it. Pile off and line up."

On the wooden shore about a small railway station he lined them up and called the roll. A sign on the station read: SAVAGE, MINN. There was a sharpness of spruce and pine in the night air, and overhead the stars were tiny lights swimming in ink. The strangeness and the cold brushed goose-flesh over Jerry's arms.

Some trucks waited behind the station, and when the roll call was completed the noncom growled, "Fall out and climb in the trucks."

Carrying their suitcases, the Niseis mounted the big, canvas-topped trucks. The engines started with a shattering noise, and one behind the other, like circus elephants, they paraded from the station down the narrow main street of a small town. A few night lights burned in the stores. Beyond the town the road became a long aisle through dense pine woods. Now and then a light, lonely and mysterious, showed briefly in the forest as the trucks roared by.

At last they swung into a lighted gateway in a wire fence. A sentry challenged the trucks; then they rolled on past some small, dark buildings to stop on the edge of what resembled a baseball diamond.

The trainees dismounted and lined up on a small parade ground.

A noncom carrying a clipboard signed something one of the drivers handed him. The trucks rolled away and the noncom stood before the trainees and gazed at them for a long time. Light from a spindly street lamp threw a long shadow behind him. He looked small, wiry, and tough.

"This is Camp Savage, Minnesota," he said out of the

corner of his mouth, and waited, as if he expected an argument. "It don't look like much, and believe me it ain't. It's an old CCC camp. I'm Sergeant Schultz. You men will bunk in 4-C. You'll be Third Platoon, C Company. Keep the noise down when we go over. Some people in this camp are trying to sleep."

Behind him, they marched to a small tar-paper barracks where lights burned. The sergeant walked with a swagger, though he was quite short, and he wore his overseas cap far down on the side of his head. As Jerry entered the barracks behind him, he caught a musty animal odor. At either side of the long room ran a row of iron cots. The building was of flimsy frame construction, with studs and rafters exposed. The air was dusty and cold.

Sergeant Schultz was speaking again in his nasal twang. "Pick yourselves a cot and stand at the foot of it."

Jerry took a cot at the near end of the room. The bed next to it was already occupied by a Japanese who apparently had been in camp for a day or two; clothing hung from nails in the wall behind him, and he lay in bed gazing sleepily at the others as they moved about. Jerry stood where he had been told, waiting. There was something ferocious about Sergeant Schultz. His black eyes snapped and his mouth had a permanent, jeering pull at one corner of it. When he spoke, it was out of this corner of his mouth and with a motion of his jaws as though he were chewing tough meat. His clean suntan uniform was freshly starched and the chevrons on it were as black and distinct as eyebrows.

"All right, you guys!" he said suddenly, in a low, menacing growl. "It don't take all night to pick out a cot. You got sheets and blankets on your beds. Now, I'm going to show you how to make a bed, and after that you better know how. You'll stand inspection every morning. Here's how you make a bed with hospital corners. . . ."

He selected Jerry's cot to make the demonstration on, laying a sheet on the thin mattress and showing them how to tuck the ends so tightly that nothing short of a crane could tear them loose. He threw on a blanket and snapped it taut as a drumhead. Then he rolled the other blanket just so and laid it across the end of the cot. Jerry was almost too tired and sleepy to keep his eyes open, but he was delighted that his bed was made, while the other men were just beginning, with great difficulty, to make theirs. The Army's patented hospital corners were hard to duplicate.

"You got it now?" Sergeant Schultz demanded. Everyone nodded, though their finished jobs were lumpy. The sergeant grinned crookedly at Jerry. "I wouldn't think of cheating you out of your practice, Private—"

With one hand, he methodically ripped the bed apart and left sheets and blankets on the floor. Some of the others laughed, and the sergeant smilingly walked to their cots and pulled their beds apart too.

"Okay, I want to see all those beds made five minutes after you roll out in the morning. The whistle will blow at four forty-five. That gives you a solid four hours of sleep tonight."

But Jerry did not sleep much. During the night he heard a gnawing, and looked down to see the vague form of a large rat chewing on one of his shoes. He struck at it and it scurried away. From time to time he heard other men striking at rats with shoes. Shortly after he'd dozed off, an uncontrollable itching woke him. He threw back the covers and tried to see the back of his knee where something was biting him.

Next to him, the Nisei who had been in bed when the platoon arrived was going over the underside of his cot with a burning match. There would be a *pop* and a little sizzling flare every so often.

"What are you doing?" Jerry asked him curiously.

"Killing bedbugs," the Nisei said. "These old barns haven't been used in so long they're full of bedbugs and rats. Help yourself to the matches on the bed. . . ."

Breakfast, like their arrival, took place in the dark.

Dawn was still far away when they were marched to the mess hall. Cafeteria-style, they lined up in the glare of naked light bulbs and carried their trays past cooks who ladled food onto them. The meal consisted of burned toast under a pale paste of creamed hamburger. It seemed to Jerry that the worst thing that could happen to good hamburger was to be drowned in flour and water.

They sat at tables for twelve and tried to eat the food.

There were aluminum pitchers of bluish milk and black coffee. The man who had been roasting bedbugs pushed his food away after a few bites.

"If I'd known we were up for creamed hamburger again, I'd have saved those bedbugs," he said.

He was a big corpulent man of about twenty-two, with a tan, pudgy face and a round head. His movements were almost lazy, and he spoke English with a complete absence of accent.

"How long have you been here?" asked Jerry.

"Five days. I've read all the mysteries in camp, and now I'm working on Sergeant Schultz's mail-order catalogue." He offered his hand. "Katsuma Komura—call me Kats."

"Jerry Harada. Glad to know you, Kats. What camp are you from?"

"Tule Lake. I was selling insurance in San Francisco before the war. You guys are from Topaz, aren't you?"

"That's right. I lived in Compton, near L.A."

"Well, we'll probably get down to work, now. A lieutenant brought in a bunch from Manzanar yesterday. That's him, now," he said, nodding at a very tall officer who had just entered the mess hall. He smiled. "He must be trying to be democratic—a Caucasian officer eating with Japanese enlisted men!"

With a warm tingle, Jerry watched Russ glance about the room as if looking for him. He raised his hand and Russ saw him and came toward their table.

"That's Lieutenant Bennett," Jerry told Kats. "I've

known him most of my life. He was a neighbor of ours. He speaks almost as much Japanese as I do."

Russ stooped across the long table from Jerry. The other Niseis looked at him in surprise. Seeing his lieutenant's bars, they started to rise, but Russ shook his head. "At ease. I'm just a dogface like the rest of you while we're in training. If nobody's sitting here, I'll take this place."

He procured his food and sat down and looked at it. He ate a few bites and pushed it away from him. "We're going to miss that mess sergeant," he sighed.

Kats leaned toward him. "I'll tell you a secret. He was a steam fitter in Duluth before he joined the army."

A rugged-looking boy named Ben Sugeta, sitting down the table a few places, asked, "What's the scoop on this ATIS deal, Lieutenant? Where are we gonna go when we finish here?"

"All over the Pacific, probably. Every place where there are Japanese enemies, we've got to have Japanese interpreters."

"When do we start training?" Jerry asked him.

"Don't get in a rush," Russ advised. "Once it starts, you won't have time to draw a deep breath. First thing, though, we draw our equipment. Then we'll get shots, buy life insurance, and take aptitude tests. After you think you're too bushed to take another test or have another shot—then the training will start in earnest, just as though you'd been resting up for it."

He told Jerry he was bunking with the First Platoon,

down the line of barracks—platoons were made up according to height, here at Savage. "But we'll probably be in some of the same classes."

After breakfast they mopped the barracks and cleaned the latrine. Jerry was given a can of water and a rag and told to clean off the window sills. It did not seem to make much improvement. Standing at a window, he looked out over the camp. Savage had an air of self-pity, of dejection, a nobody-cares-for-me look. Rusty stovepipes projected above each ridgepole at odd angles. The parade ground, long unused, was overgrown with weeds. Suddenly a whistle blew, and Jerry jumped to attention. Sergeant Schultz was standing just inside the barracks.

"Fall out and line up!"

They marched to a building where a captain explained the Army's insurance plan. Then they marched to the supply room, where each man drew uniforms, a mess kit, an old rifle, and a bayonet. While they were trying to arrange their belongings neatly in their footlockers, the whistle blew again.

"Fall out without your shirts!" the sergeant ordered.

Shirtless, they marched to the dispensary and slowly filed inside. Kats Komura stood in front of Jerry in the long line moving by inches through the small building. Behind him stood Kenny Yasui, who was barely five feet tall. Within the dispensary there was a sickening odor of alcohol and medicines. As Jerry moved through a door into the small surgery he saw with dismay what was happening. It made him think of calves being run through a slaughter-house.

On either side of the line stood a doctor stabbing needles into the arms of the recruits, so rapidly that it seemed quite possible he might inoculate the same man twice. Medics with trays of fresh needles and syringes stood by like caddies. Another man was breaking little glass vials and scratching the skin of the biceps of each man in line with the broken glass. Near the far door a medic with an instrument like a knife crossbred with a hypodermic syringe was stabbing the tip of the men's fingers and drawing off a few drops of blood onto a glass slide.

In the room there was a low, tongueless moaning. At first Jerry was puzzled to locate the source of it. Then he saw that at least a dozen men were sitting around the walls on flimsy chairs, their heads between their knees. Some of them were barely able to sit on the chairs; these were the men who were making the noises. They had fainted when they saw the needles.

For a moment he was queasy himself—all those shots within a few seconds!—two shots in one arm, one shot in the other, a vaccination, and then a stabbed finger to round it off!

Kats Komura turned and looked at him pastily. "Kinda—makes you—" he began, and then he slumped into Jerry's arms. Jerry caught and tried to support the man, but

Kats was heavy. While he was struggling with his bulk, Kenny Yasui exhaled windily, behind him, and slumped forward onto Jerry's back. Jerry was forced to his knees.

"Hey! Somebody—give me a hand!" he called weakly.

A couple of medics moved in unhurriedly. They dragged the men to a pair of empty chairs and shoved their heads down between their knees to restore circulation to the brain. One of them regarded Kats curiously.

"I don't know what it is about needles that gives some guys the willies," he said to Jerry. "Well, if that's the worst that ever happens to them—" He shrugged, and went back to his work.

That night they turned in early. Jerry was not able to sleep at once, and because he was awake longer than the others he became the witness of a phenomenon only slightly less memorable than a view of the northern lights: the enormous snoring of thirty feverish, exhausted trainees

CHAPTER 7

# The Gopher Emblem

By morning, the men's arms were so stiff and sore from the series of shots that every man in the barracks groaned as he tried to dress. None of them seriously expected to be asked to train that day. But despite their misery, they fell out in the cold dawn and went through twenty minutes of exercises on the parade ground. Their moans made the area sound like a hospital's recovery room. At one point, Sergeant Schultz had his men extend both arms sidewise, drop two-thirds of the way into a deep-knee bend, and hold it while he turned his back on them and talked for a full minute with another drill sergeant.

After breakfast they were given fifteen minutes to shave, prepare for inspection, and line up. "You guys had a good rest yesterday," the sergeant smilingly told Jerry's platoon, "and I hope you're all feeling rested. Because now we go to work. . . ."

There was a low moan from the platoon, and Schultz angrily blew his whistle. Pointing his finger at them, he warned, "I'm going to tell you jokers something, and don't you ever forget it: when that whistle blows, you line up, button up, and shut up. Is that clear?"

The sergeant glared a moment longer, and added, "I see half of you haven't buttoned your shirt pockets. Those buttons are to use, not just for the laundry to tear off. Next man I catch with a button undone gets extra duty. We're going over to the rec-hall, now, and get the load on why you're here and what'll be expected of you. Major Morris will tell you the story—he's the camp C.O. Any questions?"

Under a sky of cold, aluminum-colored clouds, they marched in two silent lines to the recreation hall. Jerry had a sad and homesick feeling that he was marching away from a life he had loved into another that might bring anything—excitement, monotony, adventure, death. And glancing at the faces of the other men, he knew they were all feeling the same way—as though they were hurrying to catch a ship which might take them anywhere, and would probably never bring them back.

Major Morris spoke for ten minutes, and spoiled the day. He was a short, capable-appearing man with tightly waved iron-gray hair which fitted his head like a cap. His full cheeks and heavy jaws were somewhat simian.

"As of this moment," he said, "only three per cent of you men are qualified linguists. We'll do the best we can with you. But, unfortunately, a lot of you won't make the grade."

He explained that the Americanization of the Japanese in this country had proceeded faster than anyone had realized. "In a lot of Japanese-American families, Japanese is seldom spoken by the younger members of the family. On top of that, the Army's definition of a linguist includes familiarity with Japanese military terms. If I were to hand each of you a captured field order right now, no more than six men in this hall could translate it correctly."

The silence became heavier and more depressed. But then the major smiled crisply.

"Of course, that's what you're here for—to learn these things. Plus some others—and that's where the shoe's going to pinch. There's more to learn than a man starting from scratch can possibly manage in six months. You'll study Japanese history and culture—so that if a prisoner you're interrogating refers to the 'divine wind,' you won't think he's going to fly a kite: he's a member of the suicide force. You'll memorize the Japanese order of battle—how many regiments in a division, how many privates in a squad and so on. You'll study their tactics and soldier psychology."

He looked down, turned over a card he held in his hand and looked up once more with an air almost of sympathy.

"Those who make it—the top language students—will be assigned immediately to combat outfits. While you're here, you'll all wear the Gopher Emblem, designed by one of our earlier graduates. Whether it becomes something to be proud of or ashamed of will depend on the men who wear it. You know as well as I do that you'll be subject to special risks that the ordinary rifleman won't. Capture by the enemy wouldn't be pleasant, I'm afraid, and despite what you may have heard, the Army doesn't issue suicide pills to be taken if you're captured."

Jerry's stomach gave a little squeeze of fear. Major Morris glanced ruefully about the interior of the ancient building.

"I wish we could make you more comfortable here, but the ration per man is less than that of a man in a federal prison. . . . We'll have to do the best we can. Good luck."

Filing out, the men were silent. But already the depression they had felt was taking the color of determination. Jerry knew this because he was Japanese himself—aware of how their minds worked. The Japanese were a proud people—too proud for their own good sometimes. The men were strenuously competitive in business, working night and day to outdo their competitors. When a Japanese boy dropped from an *A* to a *B* in a subject, his father would say, "Ah, so! Hinoki's son received an *A*, but my own lazy son got a *B* because he wasted time collecting butterflies! How will you look before your friends?" So the Nisei sheepishly put away his butterfly net and got back to work.

Perhaps Major Morris knew that. He wanted the men to study hard, so he applied what leverage he knew. Or perhaps it was all true—many of them would fail.

That night Jerry got out the camera his parents had given him. He had a strong intuition that after tonight there would not be time for such unessential activities as picture-taking—and butterfly-collecting. He stood on his footlocker and called down the long barracks where men were polishing shoes and cleaning brass for inspection.

"Attensh-*hut!*" he said, mimicking Sergeant Schultz.

He grinned as they all snapped to attention. Seeing him, some of the men grumbled and began returning to their work, but Jerry called quickly, "Wait a minute! How about a picture of you guys? I'll get prints for everybody."

"When they see this gang, they'll think you're in prison," Kats predicted. Men began drifting down to the end of the barracks where Jerry was waiting.

Pulling three footlockers together, he made a long bench where six men could sit, while six others stood behind. He knelt before the group and raised the miniature camera to his eye. The men took positions, looking very noble and serious.

"Hold steady, now—" he said.

"*As you were!*"

A harsh voice slashed the quiet like an ax. With a start, Jerry looked around. Sergeant Schultz stood in the doorway to the small squad room where he bunked. Hands on hips, the grim little Arkansan walked forward with his small-man's swagger and put out his hand.

"Let's have it."

"The camera?" Jerry said, coming to his feet.

"The camera, soldier."

Jerry looked at it. A flush of anger heated him. Right or wrong, Schultz had no call to come barging in and humiliate him before his friends. Kats, Yasui, and the others were still standing stiffly like figures in an old-fashioned photograph, afraid to move.

"I don't get it," he said.

"Cameras aren't allowed on this post. Didn't anybody ever tell you that?"

"No. They didn't."

"I'm tellin' you now, Harada. Let's have it."

Jerry's hands clenched on the camera and he glared at the sergeant. Schultz waited while Jerry fought his own stubbornness, hating to back down, to be made a fool of; but finally he handed over the camera.

Examining it, Sergeant Schultz rubbed his jaw. "Nice little camera. I'll turn it in to the orderly room. They may give it back when you ship out." He walked away, but at the door to the squad room, he looked back.

"Reveille's at five o'clock. If I was you characters, I'd get in the habit of shaving at night—you won't have time in the morning. Bed-check at nine-thirty from now on—and you better hit the sack when you hear the bugles play 'Quarters!"

After the lights were out, Kats muttered from his cot, "That was too bad, Jerry. What harm could a camera do in a beat-up old camp like this? It's not like tar-paper shacks were a military secret."

"I'll get those pictures," Jerry said doggedly.

"Without a camera?"

"One way or another."

He could hear Kats turning to look at him. "How?"

"I don't know, yet."

His mind was handling the problem curiously, willingly accepting the task Schultz had set it. He was determined to get the pictures, because Schultz had made a fool of him. By getting the pictures, he would make a fool of Schultz. But how could he get them without a camera?

In a high-school science course he had studied photography. He remembered that a camera is, basically, a very simple mechanism: a closed box (or "chamber," the translation of the Latin word *camera*) with a hole in it through which light rays enter and are focused on a piece of film. That was all the early *camera obscura* consisted of: a box with a photographic emulsion in the back of it and a hole in the front. But some kind of shutter and lens were required, too. Where was he going to get a shutter and lens? It was a problem, all right. But he was determined to solve it.

## CHAPTER 8

# Pride of a Nisei

Battleships went through brutal shakedown cruises, Jerry had heard, and in a way that was what happened to the would-be Intelligence and Reconnaissance men during the next few weeks.

They adapted themselves to the inferior food, devised methods of trapping rats, and waged savage warfare on the bedbugs; but they never got accustomed to the man-killing work load. They went through their textbook a quarter-inch at a time, studying, memorizing, struggling through tests. The endless studying was like a tropical fever, prolonged and enervating, which burned up all the energy of one's body, and then seared the mind so that it was scarred and almost impervious to learning. They dragged from one class to another. Men began dropping out, hopelessly behind—intelligent men, too, but without sufficient background in the Japanese language to keep up.

Near the end of each day, Jerry would go to *sosho* class, but would find himself unable to recall at the end of the period characters he had memorized at the beginning. They lay on the page like bits of dried and twisted grass, attractive but perfectly meaningless. They would begin to move as he looked at them—tiny stick-men and animals, little houses with peaked roofs, weird insects that crawled into the white spaces between the columns of type.

In the class in Japanese military arts, he would lecture himself severely for having forgotten what he had learned the day before. Without mercy for his stupidity he would drill it into his mind again:

". . . The Japanese usually attack just before dawn, because men are tired then. . . . A Japanese trailblock is set up in an S-pattern, with machine guns placed so that . . ."

But when he reviewed it that evening before 'Quarters sounded, he would find he had forgotten nearly all of it.

The one cheerful time of day was Mail Call.

After lunch, Sergeant Schultz would step into the barracks and bawl, "Mail Call!" Then he would begin calling off names from the packet of letters he held. The Niseis sat on their bunks to read their mail, hungry to know how it went with their friends and relatives in the relocation centers. They prolonged the fun by reading portions of their letters to one another. Jerry received pictures of his family taken by a friend at Topaz. While he was fitting the snapshots into his wallet, Kats picked up the picture of Helen.

"Miss Little Tokyo, eh? Going to introduce me after the war?"

"It won't do any good," Jerry kidded him. "She likes thin men."

He was relieved when his father wrote that he was now

working outside the center in the beet fields. It was hard work, but Japanese farmers were accustomed to hard work. It brought in some money and kept him from brooding over the sad change in their life.

Late in the summer the weather began to change. There were frequent cold rains. One night a wind blew monstrously through the forest, trying every seam and crack in the old buildings, so that by morning the men were more than ready to leave their chilly beds and get into warm clothing. At the end of the long room was a small cast-iron stove. Jerry found some newspapers and made a fire. The papers were damp and slow to catch. He stood there warming his hands and watching a margin of brown retreat before the thin blue flame moving across the paper. Giving off little heat, it ate across a display advertisement for Kermit's Market, consuming the mayonnaise special ("one to a customer"), lamb patties, and curling now around fig bars ("*U No the Brand!*") at eleven cents. There was little warmth, either, in fig bars, but his attention was caught by a vision of the familiar box, and as though a button had been pushed, facts began to tabulate themselves in his mind.

At last he knew where he was going to get his camera.

That weekend he went into town on a six-hour pass with a truckload of other trainees. Russ was able to get away also. He was looking haggard and run-down from the endless study and the brief nights of rest. They walked down the sidewalk of the main street, feeling momentarily a great sense of release.

"Man, if I ever get through this," Russ said, "I'm going to find a nice oak tree in California and just lie in the shade the rest of my life."

"*Do no kurai guntai ni orimasu ka?*" Jerry said, grinning. ("How long have you been in the service?")

"Quiet," Russ said. "Only English is spoken here."

Jerry found Kermit's Market. The proprietor watched Jerry curiously as they moved among the islanded displays. Jerry selected a box of fig bars and a roll of friction tape. He carried them to the cash register. Uncertain whether to be friendly, the market owner took his money and rang up the sale.

"Say, what nationality are you, son?" he asked bluntly. "I've seen a lot of you boys around town lately. Some of the folks claim you look kind of Japanesey."

"We're Weetonkas," Jerry said soberly.

"What's that?"

"It's a Florida Indian tribe. All us young bucks enlisted at the same time."

"Well, land o' Goshen! What you fellas doing 'way up here in Minnesota?"

"We're not supposed to talk about it," Jerry said, lowering his voice. "I can tell you this much, though—we're going to submarine school."

"*Submarine school!* A thousand miles from the ocean?"

"We're just studying instruments here. Then we'll go —no, I'd better not tell you any more. . . . You don't have any thirty-five millimeter camera film, do you?"

The storekeeper looked impressed. "No, sorry. Did you try the drugstore?"

"I'll check there."

As he and Russ left, they heard the man confiding to someone. "Hey, Joe—they're Indians, that's what! I told you they weren't Japs!"

At the drugstore, Jerry bought a cartridge of black-and-white camera film. For another quarter, the druggist sold him an empty cartridge.

"What's that combination supposed to equal?" Russ scoffed. "Fig bars, friction tape, and camera film."

"Tell you sometime," Jerry said cryptically.

Russ frowned at him. "Wait a minute!" he said suddenly. "If you're inventing some kind of camera, take it easy. Cameras aren't allowed on the post."

"You're telling me! Schultz took mine away from me the first time I took it out of my footlocker. What a lot of bunk! What have we got at Savage that the enemy would want a picture of?"

Russ shrugged. "All I know is, there are three ways of doing things—the right way, the wrong way, and the Army way. If the Army wants to fight the war without cameras, it's not up to us to show them where they're wrong."

The faint rebuke in his voice made Jerry stubborn. "I'm not trying to. I just want to see whether it can be done." And make a fool of Schultz! his mind added.

That night Jerry waited until Sergeant Schultz left the squadroom, his cap carefully cocked over one eye. Obviously he was going to town on a pass. Jerry went to work.

Stripping the wrapping from the box of cookies, he punched a pinhole in the bottom of the carton. He removed the wax-paper liner. Then, opening the box, he stretched the wax paper tightly over it. He held the box up to the ceiling light, and his heart gave a little drumbeat of triumph. He could see the inverted image of the light globe reflected through the pinhole onto the wax paper! The pinhole acted as a primitive lens: even the focus was reasonably sharp.

Hurriedly—a book close at hand in case an officer should enter on a surprise inspection—Jerry pulled the leader from the cartridge of film. He fed the end of the leader into the empty cartridge. With friction tape, he secured a cartridge at either end of the box. Then he closed the box and sealed all the openings with tape. He pressed a bit of tape over the pinhole to protect the film until he was ready to make his exposure.

By inserting the blade of his penknife through the box and into the end of the take-up cartridge, he was able to use it like a key to advance the film. He was ready!

"Hey, Kats," he called softly.

Kats's tan Buddha-face appeared above the book he was reading: *Dictionary of Japanese Military Terms.*

"Hold still," Jerry said. "I'm taking your picture."

Kats sat up, staring at the box in Jerry's lap. "What are you talking about?"

"Sit still—just like you are."

Kats froze, his gaze on the cookie box. An expression of consternation grew in his eyes. When Jerry sat back, he asked in a whisper, "You mean you've got a *camera* in that!"

"I mean this *is* a camera! All a camera is is a lens, a box, and a piece of film. A pinhole will refract light just like a lens—only not so clearly. The pinhole throws the picture onto the film at the back of the box. Then I advance it like this—" He inserted the blade of his penknife and gave the take-up spool a couple of turns.

Kats rocked his head. "And if Schultz catches on, boy, you're in trouble!"

"He won't catch on. I'm going to keep it hidden in the ventilator." Jerry glanced up at the sheet-metal ventilator above his bunk. "After I get some more pictures," he added.

"For gosh sakes, Jerry! What are you trying to prove?"

"Nothing. I'm just trying to get some pictures."

Jerry moved down to Yasui's cot. Kenny was lying down with a book, murmuring to himself in Japanese. "Hey," Jerry said. "Smile!"

Kenny gazed at him blankly.

"I'm taking your picture," Jerry explained.

"How?" The little Nisei frowned, then began to grin. He sat very still. Jerry steadied himself for a few moments against a supporting post.

"Prints will be available next week," he said.

He took a picture of every man in the platoon that night. The next day, Sunday, as Sergeant Schultz was standing in the sunlight talking to another noncom, Jerry got a picture of him through a window. He wanted to leave a print for the sergeant to find after he had shipped out. Then he hid the camera in the ventilator above his bed. Next weekend he would leave the film in town for developing.

The weather suddenly turned cold, the sky massing with packs of dark clouds as a storm gathered, a wind roughing the tops of the pines. One morning they looked out and saw the ground whitened with an inch of snow. The sergeant came from his room wearing a field jacket and gloves.

"So now it's snowing," he announced disgustedly. "And the danged coal hasn't shown up yet!"

"What'll we do for heat?"

"I'll try to promote some fuel oil. There's a furnace in this henhouse, if I can get it to work. I'm telling you for sure—this is the worst penny-pinching outfit I was ever in!"

"What was the best?" Jerry asked him.

Schultz said bitterly, "There's only two good outfits in the army—the one you just came from, and the one you're goin' to next."

At three o'clock, a Pfc. from the orderly room came to the classroom where Jerry had just settled himself for the class in Japanese culture. "Michio Harada," he called sternly, looking over the young men in their places. Jerry raised his hand. "C.O. wants to see you—on the double," the clerk said, and left.

The Japanese instructor smiled at Jerry. "One of our young men has been indiscreet, maybe?"

Jerry pushed his books onto a corner of the desk and left the room.

CHAPTER 9

# "Dangerous and Hazardous Duty!"

The orderly room, a small building on the parade ground, was distinguished from the other structures primarily by the blue-gray shaving of smoke curling from its chimney. Jerry entered. Feeling conspicuous and uneasy, he wondered whether one of his family was ill and he was to return to Topaz on emergency leave. A second chilling thought was that he was failing in his studies and was being transferred to a regular army camp.

At a small desk sat the camp sergeant major. He looked up as Jerry approached, a stolid, heavy-set man of middle age.

"Private Harada reporting, sergeant," Jerry said.

After a long, keen stare, the sergeant said, "Major Morris wants to talk to you, Harada."

"What's up?" Jerry asked.

The sergeant major rapped his pencil on the desk. "Let's let him tell you."

With his thumb, he indicated an open door behind him, with a small sign above it:

MAJOR MORRIS
CAMP COMMANDER

Jerry walked to the door, straightened his tie, checked his buttons, and prepared to knock. At a long desk almost bare of papers and furnishings sat the camp commander, his elbows supporting his weight as he methodically signed papers and turned them over in a neat pile. Shock hit Jerry numbingly as he saw a small cardboard box placed conspicuously in the middle of the desk. It had been reinforced with strips of black friction tape; the top of it was open and an empty film cartridge lay beside it. . . . It was his homemade camera.

*Oh, Lord!* he groaned.

Sergeant Schultz had probably been examining the ventilators in preparation for turning the furnace on, checking for rats and for mouse-nests, which were found everywhere.

Jerry stood there with his face and ears turning red—the only part of his body still warm. He felt cold and weak as he waited to be recognized. The major continued signing papers. Jerry rapped cautiously and the C.O. glanced at him across his glasses and resumed his work.

*What now?* Jerry wondered. After a few moments he entered and stood rigidly at attention before the desk. The C.O. did not look up. Jerry brought his hand up in a crisp salute.

Without acknowledging him, Major Morris said dryly, "I don't remember telling you to come in."

"Sir, I thought—when you looked at me—"

"You'd better go out and start over again."

Limply, Jerry let his hand fall, did a left-face, and marched out, coldly furious with the knowledge that he had been trapped. From all parts of the orderly room, he felt the eyes of clerks upon him, savoring his humiliation. He knocked again and waited. Major Morris' hand continued to describe graceful motions above the papers like the figures made by an ice-skater. Again Jerry rapped, the blood in his face hot and angry.

At last the major murmured, "Come in."

Jerry walked in. The C.O. returned his salute. Then he picked up the homemade camera and examined it curiously.

"Quite an ingenious device, actually."

"Thank you, sir."

"Oh, don't thank me. I only meant that it's the most ingenious method of getting court-martialed that I've ever come across."

"Court-martialed, sir?" Jerry repeated weakly.

The major's gaze pried at him. "You knew it was against the rules, didn't you?"

"Yes, sir, but—it seemed like such a pointless rule. I didn't see what harm a few pictures could do."

From a drawer, the major took a little sheaf of photographs and began glancing through them. "I had the film developed. Were these for your own uses, or for transmittal to the enemy?"

"I don't see how they'd help the enemy much, sir," Jerry replied.

"Don't you really? Some of our graduates may be landed in Japan proper, by parachute or from submarines. Now, suppose the Japanese counterespionage agents have photographs of them? If some of these men apply for jobs in Japanese plants, with the eventual aim of sabotaging them—isn't it almost certain they'd eventually be spotted as American agents?"

Jerry's knees began to tremble. "I guess so, sir. But these were just pictures I was going to give the boys to send home!"

Spreading the small prints out on his desk like a poker hand, Morris glanced over them. "What strikes me as particularly suspicious is that there is just one man in the platoon whose picture you *didn't* take—almost as though you were protecting him."

"Sir? Whose is that?" Jerry asked.

"Your own," the major said, staring at him. "That's how we knew who had taken the pictures."

Jerry felt imprisoned in a large cube of ice—unable to think or move.

"How do you explain that?" the C.O. prodded.

"I forgot!" Jerry confessed. "I got so involved in trying to work out the camera that after I got it made, I—I forgot to have somebody take my own picture!"

The major leaned back. "You've come pretty close to having your picture taken, though, Harada—with your head shaved and a number on your chest. I've looked into your file. You were an amateur radio operator, weren't you?"

". . . Yes, sir."

"Did you ever have occasion to talk by radio with Japanese agents disguised as tuna fishermen?"

Jerry gazed at the major steadily. "No, sir," he said quietly. "I may be Oriental, but I'm a loyal American."

"Are you?" Major Morris countered. "That's what we've been trying to establish. For all your having been born and raised in the United States, you're still Japanese, aren't you?"

"No, sir," Jerry replied.

The major raised his eyebrows. "Oh? You mean your parents are Japanese, but you aren't?"

"None of us are, sir. We're Americans of Japanese ancestry."

Morris pondered it, and then smiled. He began thoughtfully gathering up the photographs. " 'Americans of Japanese ancestry,' " he reflected. "I like that. Because that's exactly what this whole program is predicated on—our faith that you may look Oriental, but you think and act American. I had a little talk with your platoon sergeant about you," he said. "Also with your company commander and Lieutenant Bennett."

"Yes, sir?" Jerry said stiffly.

Morris tore the pictures across. "Schultz says you're a

good man, if a bit too inquisitive for your own good. You know, there are two words that will get you in a great deal of trouble, Harada. I'm afraid you're already overly familiar with them."

"What are they, sir?"

"*What if*," the major said.

Jerry gazed at him. "What if?"

" 'What if I made a camera from a cookie box?' 'What if I plugged up my rifle barrel so it wouldn't get dusty between inspections?' Of course this is a very useful trait—curiosity. But it needs to be carefully controlled—like a bonfire."

He dropped the pictures in the wastebasket. "At any rate, Captain Curdy gives you a good report, as does Lieutenant Bennett. Bennett says he's known you most of his life and regards you as at least as American as the Statue of Liberty. Do you agree with that estimate?"

"At least, sir," Jerry replied faintly.

The major glanced past him and raised his voice. "Sergeant Broom!" The sergeant major appeared in the doorway. "Inform Sergeant Schultz that Harada is to have KP for the next two weeks. He will not leave the post for two months. Of course," he told Jerry, "you can ask for a court-martial, if you prefer."

"No, sir," Jerry said. He felt as though a bottle of soda water had been uncapped in him and the bubbles were rising through him. Heady with relief, he said, "Thank you, sir! I promise not to get in trouble again."

"I wonder," the major said. "Curiosity like yours isn't easily harnessed. It makes Edisons out of some men, and gets the rest in trouble. It all depends on whether you run it, or it runs you."

An almost arctic cold flowed over the country like a glacier, freezing everything before it, draining the blue from the sky and making the ground as hard and dry as iron. Still there was no coal for the stoves, no oil for the furnaces. Work parties cut wood in the forest, but the fuel was green and difficult to start. The trainees lived in overcoats, piling all their clothing on their cots to keep warm at night.

Yet, to Jerry's great satisfaction, there was no sense of resentment among the men. They hated the cold, disliked the food, fought the vermin, but did not whisper to one another, "Because we are Japanese, they are doing this to us!" They said, "Because there are ignorant men in Washington, we must get along the best we can." Some day the ignorant men would be made wiser—perhaps by the record of the young wearers of the Gopher Emblem.

And then, suddenly, the training was over.

It was like a moving picture ending. The lights came up and they sat there numbed by the work they had just completed, and waited to be told what to do next. For two days they sat around the barracks or strolled the frozen paths, waiting it out. One morning there was a special formation. Sergeant Broom, the sergeant major, read from a long list.

" 'Following enlisted men will assemble here at eleven hundred hours with full equipment: Asami, Shigeru. Akahita, Hideo. . . .' "

Jerry's spirits fell as the *H*'s were passed and his name was not called. But after the roster had been read, the sergeant major shuffled some papers and read from another.

" 'Following men will report to the orderly room at the conclusion of this formation: Bennett, Russell. Harada, Michio. Sugeta, Ben. . . .' "

Fourteen men walked to the orderly room and waited for Major Morris to appear. Sergeant Broom worked at his desk as though this were any other workday. After a few minutes, the commander's door opened and he returned the Niseis' salute. "Will you men come into my office?"

Crowded into the little room, they waited for him to speak. With amusement, Jerry glanced at the faces of the other men—at Hank Gosho, Ben Sugeta, and Roy Matsumoto. Talk about Oriental inscrutability! Every man in the room was glowing like a vacuum tube.

"You men," the major began, "were selected as the top candidates at Savage. I don't mean that you're the best students, necessarily. For example, Sugeta's English leaves a lot to be desired. But Matsumoto's Japanese isn't as strong as Sugeta's. Between the two of them, they make a team it would be hard to beat—Sugeta to break a soldier's slangy scrawl down into simple Japanese, Matsumoto to put it into English."

A coal crumbled in the little airtight stove in the corner. The room was soundless. Jerry was breathing shallowly with anticipation.

"You're being asked to volunteer for a dangerous mission. I can't tell you what it is, but take my word for it you won't sleep under a roof very often. Any takers?"

Jerry raised his hand quickly. Sugeta's arm went up, and in a moment every man's hand was raised. Major Morris chuckled.

"Don't you want to know any more about it than that?"

"No, sir," most of the men said quickly.

"That's it, then!" said the C.O. "You'll leave here tonight. Don't try to take any non-government issue—they'll just take it away at the port of embarkation. Anything you want to send home, wrap it and leave it at the orderly room. Including cameras and fig bars. . . ."

Everyone smiled at Jerry.

## CHAPTER 10

# "Operation Sextant"

For once the Army seemed to be in a hurry.

Jerry and the thirteen other volunteers arrived at Camp Stoneman, California, forty-eight hours after they left Savage. Stoneman was the port of embarkation for San Francisco. The camp was a mournful city of ugly barracks near the wide and murky San Joaquin River. All residents of Stoneman, except the permanent cadre, were temporary. A round of medical and dental examinations followed. Equipment was issued and special inoculations administered. While thousands of other soldiers destined for duty in the Pacific played poker, read, and killed time as best they could, the Niseis were rushed from one place to the next.

At every spare moment, they wrote the letters they knew they might not get written for weeks, once they were in combat. Their platoon sergeant told them they were the letter-writingest outfit he had ever seen.

One night Yasui looked up from his tablet with a frown. "How do you spell *battalion?*" he asked Jerry.

"Two *t*'s and one *l*. You mean you're writing your folks in English?"

"Sure."

"Your folks can *read* English?" asked Eddie Mitsukado.

"A little. Not much," Yasui admitted.

"Now I've heard everything," Russ said with a laugh. "They only read Japanese, so he writes them in English!"

Yasui inspected the tip of his fountain pen. "Well, my sister reads English, and she translates for them. That way they can kind of flap my letters in their friends' faces and say, 'We get letter from Kenny. He says Army is fine. His letter all in English. Oh, and how is your son Stanley coming with his language studies? Can he make English letters yet?' "

The others laughed; but Jerry had a warm feeling around his heart. These parents of theirs, with their desire to be one hundred per cent American and their touching pride in their sons' and daughters' progress in citizenship—he was very proud of them. For the old Japanese knew that they themselves would never learn good English—that difficult language of rules-to-be-broken and compound inconsistencies. All their hopes for a sound linguistic reputation were centered on their children, and they sacrificed everything to give them the kind of education they could never have had in Japan.

One night the order came through attaching them to the 5307th Composite Unit (Provisional)—whatever that was. Russ was called to a meeting of officers. He returned to the barracks with exciting news.

"We ship out in the morning! I don't know where to, but there'll be three thousand men in the outfit, and it'll be split up into three battalions. We're to be attached to the battalion Intelligence and Reconnaissance platoons. The Five-three-oh-seventh will be part of a bigger unit called 'Galahad Force.' There'll be four of us in each battalion and two in headquarters. I'll be assigned to Second Battalion, along with Jerry, Matsumoto, and Sugeta. Okay, let's pack!"

Next day they marched to a wharf and boarded a riverboat for San Francisco. That night they left the boat and marched up the gangplank of a troop transport. Jerry had a good look at some of the men they would be fighting with. He was reminded of brigands. For the most part, the soldiers were cold-eyed, seasoned-looking men with a go-to-the-devil air. He himself was queasy at the thought of sailing from the United States—perhaps to his death. His mind dwelt on the possibility of submarine attack; he thought bleakly of death from wounds or disease in some jungle. But these men shuffled down the deck with their barracks bags over their shoulders as though they had little interest in where they were going.

At daybreak the ship moved softly from her slip. Through a fog wine-colored with dawn, she slipped silently under the Golden Gate Bridge onto the open sea. Jerry and Russ stood at the rail. Gradually Jerry became aware of a soldier standing at the other side of him. He looked at him and saw a short, stocky man with the battered face of a boxer. There was scar tissue over his pale blue eyes and his nose seemed to have been set slightly to one side. The man looked him over hostilely.

"What the hell you doing here?" he demanded.

Jerry returned his stare. "I'm with the 5307th. What's your excuse?"

"Me? I joined up to fight Japs. When I get off this boat, I'm going to start the biggest collection of Jap ears in the Pacific. How 'bout that?"

Jerry smiled. "You don't have to wait that long, soldier. Take mine."

Russ stepped back so that the other man could see his lieutenant's bars. "As you were—both of you," he said. "What's your name, Private?"

"Crane," the man said. "What's yours, Lieutenant—'long as we're getting acquainted?"

"Bennett. I've got news for you, Crane. When we get in combat, our lives may depend on the Niseis in our outfit. Maybe you didn't know that."

Crane's gaze traveled over Jerry. "I sure didn't, Lieutenant. How's that work, now?"

"It works like this: The only way to keep ahead of the enemy is to be able to read his documents when we capture them. But there are only fourteen men on this ship who read and speak Japanese! That should make them pretty important to us, shouldn't it?"

Crane spat over the side of the ship. "Maybe too important. How are we going to know whether they're giving us a fair translation or not?"

"We don't, but it figures. They've got as big a stake in this war as we have. Most of them grew up in the United States and were educated here. Niseis aren't Japanese as most people understand the term. They're Americans of Japanese ancestry."

"And sympathies," Crane retorted. "There only has to be one liar among them to foul an outfit up completely! Ain't that a fact?"

"Maybe. That's the risk we have to take. But the damage one disloyal man might do couldn't touch the good the others will be doing. Intelligence men have won more than one war, you know. Just for example—what would you do if you killed an enemy with a field order in his pocket? Or located a telephone line in the jungle?"

Crane grinned. "I'd probably tear up the field order and cut the telephone line."

"And throw away information that might save your own hide? Use your head, Private!" Russ said disgustedly.

A line of muscle quivered in Crane's jaws. "If we'd 'a' used our heads twenty years ago, Lieutenant, we wouldn't be in this war now! We should've gone to war with Japan in 'Thirty-seven, after they sank that gunboat of ours on the Yangtze. And while we were at it, we should have shipped every Japanese crop-picker in the U.S. back to Japan! We're the only country in the world soft enough to let spies camp on us and treat them like guests!"

Jerry's temper was rising. He moved toward Crane. "Maybe you'd better put up or shut up, soldier. Give me one case of disloyalty among the Niseis."

"I could give you fifty! I knew a guy at Camp Hood whose sister lived in Los Angeles. Her gardener had a portable transmitter in his truck, see? He was a major in the Japanese underground! When the Japs invaded, he was going to be the boss-man in the sabotage gang! They found two hundred pounds of high explosives in his basement."

"No fooling!" Jerry chuckled. "They don't have basements in Los Angeles. Sure it wasn't in the attic?"

Crane flushed. "What about all those arsenals they dug up under Japanese greenhouses after the war broke out!"

Jerry laughed. "You mean roots, don't you? My father had a greenhouse, but the only gun in it was a shotgun we used to shoot rabbits that were eating the crops."

The other man began rubbing his fist against his palm. "Keep talkin', Tojo," he said. "Somebody's going to get you straightened out pretty quick."

"All right, that's enough," Rus snapped. "Just try to understand one thing before we get where we're going. These men volunteered for hazardous duty—as you did. The difference is that if they're captured they stand a good chance of being tortured. That's not hard to understand, is it?"

Crane scratched his neck, a disdainful grin on his lips. "No, sir. That makes sense. Something else that makes sense is this—if this character ever taps a Jap telephone line, he can use it to give away our plans just as easy as he can listen in on theirs, can't he? Be thinkin' about that, Lieutenant."

He gave Russ a casual salute and drifted down the deck.

Without escort, a furtive shadow on the submarine-haunted waters, the transport thrust her prow westward across the Pacific.

The food was fair; the sleeping accommodations were crowded. The ship had once been a luxury liner plying between the West Coast and Hawaii. Her carpets had been stored and the pastel walls and carved moldings of her staterooms were protected by unpainted panels. Where two passengers had slept in comfortable beds, eight or ten men were now accommodated in tiers three bunks high. Russ shared a small stateroom with three other junior officers, while Jerry and the Niseis had a larger cabin in which fourteen of them bunked.

In a short time, monotony had taken the edge off everyone's excitement. Nothing was to be seen except the deep, purplish water stretching to a hazy horizon in all directions. Training continued, but consisted primarily of calisthenics.

One morning Jerry saw Ben Sugeta staring out a porthole. "What do you see?" he asked him.

"Nothing. I keep thinking we'll raise Hawaii one of these days."

"Is that where we're going?"

"Where else? Maybe we'll get leave at Pearl Harbor!"

But the ship did not put in at Hawaii. It towed its marbled wake across the Pacific, now in this direction, now in that, as though the rudder chains had broken.

Rolling in heavy seas, SF 1280 thrust on through gray-blue water. After more than a week the atmosphere in the cabin was growing tense. Everyone was short-tempered and bored. After dozing half the day, it was hard to sleep at night. The endless, throbbing grind of engines underfoot worked on the nerves like sandpaper. Sugeta started an elaborate carving on the stock of his M-1 rifle. Jerry stopped to look at it one morning as he sat on his bunk carving with his penknife.

*To do or die,* he read in raised letters on the walnut stock. Beneath the words were hearts pierced with an arrow. "How come no initials, Ben?" Jerry grinned.

"I don't believe in entanglements," Ben grunted. "Only foreign ones. Maybe I'll meet a girl in Australia."

"So now we're going to Australia?" Kenny Yasui asked him, looking up from a letter he was writing.

"That's what I figure. It's not going to be an island invasion, because we haven't had any landing practice. They haven't even asked if we could swim."

"What about India or Burma?"

Sugeta snapped his knife shut. "That would mean weeks on this lousy ship on this lousy ocean!" he said angrily.

Yasui capped his fountain pen. "It's better than some oceans. No icebergs, at least."

"Okay, but what's to lose by letting us know where we are?"

"As Sergeant Schultz used to say, 'When the army wants you to know something, soldier, they'll tell you.' " Jerry went over and gazed out the porthole. "I wish I could borrow a sextant somewhere."

"What's a sextant?"

"A gadget for taking bearings at sea. It looks kind of like a surveyor's transit. I used to practice with one when I was taking astronomy in high school. I got pretty good."

"How's it work?" asked Sugeta.

"Well, it's kind of complicated. If you're taking bearings in the daytime, you use the sun for a guide. You measure the angle between the sun and the horizon, and that gives you your latitude. Or if you're doing it at night, you can take three star sights, draw the angles on a map, and where they intersect is where you are."

Sugeta leaned back. He winked at Kenny Yasui. "A dollar gets you five you couldn't locate this tub within a thousand miles—not even with a crate of sextants!"

"There's nothing to it," Jerry said.

"Okay, then it's an easy five."

Kenny pulled a dollar bill from his pocket and straightened it. "I've got an easy dollar that says we're near Australia."

Hank Gosho rolled from his bunk. He was so relaxed these days that they were beginning to call him "Horizontal

Hank." "I'll take that bet, junior. And I've got another dollar that's got 'New Guinea' written on it. Somebody want to argue about that one?"

Eddie Mitsukado had been shining his shoes. He shined them so often these long days that the polish had begun to crack when he walked. Dropping the shoebrush, he thrust his hand into his pocket.

"You just lost a buck, Hank," he said. "We're near New Zealand. I had a dream about it last night."

"That was a nightmare!" Sugeta said. "Haven't you heard about the girls in New Zealand? They're all tattooed!"

"I'd settle for bearded ladies if it would get us off this ship!" Hank muttered.

Jerry listened to the bets going around. A sudden, strong desire to locate the ship seized him. He walked to the porthole and looked out over the water, a blue desert without landmarks. He was certain that he could pin down the ship's location to within a few miles—if he had a sextant. The old flame of curiosity in him—turned down to a pilot light since the camera incident—flared up.

"How about it, skipper?" Sugeta said, behind him. "Don't you want to take that easy five away from me?"

"What would I use for a sextant?"

"I don't know. But I do know that after another week of slopping around in this ocean without knowing whether we're off Greenland or India, I'm going to jump off and start swimming."

That night in the chow line, in the big cafeteria where women in evening gowns and men in dinner jackets had once filled the room with vacation chatter, Ben spoke to him in a whisper.

"I've found a sextant!"

Jerry turned quickly. "Where?"

"I sneaked up to the bridge today and looked around. It was lying on a table in the navigation room. I walked right in! I could have picked it up and walked out."

"Why didn't you look at the chart while you were there?" Jerry expostulated.

"I did. The ship's position wasn't marked on it. They must keep the working chart under lock and key." Sugeta lowered his voice. "Why don't you go up there after chow and borrow the sextant for a minute?"

Jerry rubbed his neck. He was powerfully tempted. "—I'd have to have a bubble sextant," he frowned, "or I couldn't plot anything but the latitude. At night, the bubble takes the place of the horizon, since you can't see the horizon. Were there any books around?"

"Sure, there was a whole shelf of them. Why?"

"Because I'd have to use a nautical almanac to find three bright stars and look them up in a table. How do you get up to the bridge, anyway?" he wanted to know. "I didn't think enlisted men were allowed up there?"

Ben grinned. "So I've heard. But I didn't see anybody to throw me off. Plenty of places to hide if anybody did come along." Ben pulled a five-dollar bill from his pocket and snapped it between his fingers. "How about it? Yasui says he'll bet you five, too."

Jerry thought of the Vikings, sailing the ocean with these same stars to guide them. Of Columbus and Magellan . . . and a million fishermen in little boats, relying on those same tiny chips of frosty stars to guide them home. The idea excited him—the practical application of something which had merely been theory before. He glanced back down the line of Japanese faces watching him with anticipation.

"Tell you a secret," Ben whispered. "There's at least a thousand dollars being bet on you!"

"A thousand dollars!"

"It's kind of spread out a little," Ben confided. "Sergeant Manning heard about it and wanted in on it. He bet a buddy of his that we're near the Marshalls. Then a buddy of his buddy's heard about it—and I guess it's all over the ship by now! Everybody's betting on where we are."

Jerry frowned. He was not keen for the responsibility of settling so many bets, and he was disturbed that the secret had gotten out. For the news would have traveled by enlisted man's telegraph all over the ship that some Japanese in the Intelligence Section had bragged that he could find out where they were. If he failed, every Nisei on the transport would lose face.

"Okay," he sighed. "It's a bet."

CHAPTER 11

# Man Overboard!

Jerry climbed two decks, until he was on the level just below the bridge. A sign beside the ladder read: OFFICERS' COUNTRY. Some men were coming along the rail, the ruby sparks of their cigarettes glowing. Seeing him, they halted and seemed to peer at him closely. Jerry turned quickly and gazed out over the blackness of the ocean. If he were turned in for being on the officers' deck, he might find himself on kitchen police for the rest of the voyage.

He heard the men coming on. They were not speaking. Reaching him, they continued walking, their heads down; and Jerry realized they were enlisted men, like himself, seeking a change of scenery and just as worried about his reporting them as he had been about their reporting him. They had only gone a few feet past him when one of them suddenly turned back.

"Hey, Tojo!" the GI called softly. "How you likin' the trip?"

Jerry looked around. The soldier was Crane, the man who had baited him the first morning aboard ship. He walked back to look at Jerry.

"I'm liking it fine," Jerry said.

"Me too. I'm thinking about all those Jap ears I'm going to collect. Gonna wear 'em on a string around my neck."

"You may have to fight to get them," Jerry reminded him. "Sure you won't lose your own?"

Crane's eyes were small and cocky under a bony ledge. As the other men drifted back, he stepped close to Jerry, grinning. "Hey, now! You want to try taking mine?" he said.

"No. I'll just hold onto my own."

"May take some doing. Of course, you being a Jap, you must know all about judo, huh?"

"A little."

"I know a little about boxing. Why don't we settle the old argument, huh?"

"What argument?"

"About whichun's harder to lick—a wrestler or a fighter."

Crane laid a hand on Jerry's shoulder, as if testing the muscles of it. Looking at the craggy face, Jerry knew that Crane either was or had been a professional fighter. He could see the faces of the other men, waiting with expectant grins for what would happen next. And Jerry knew he could not back down. "You know those Japs"—Crane would spread it around. "Tie a tin can to their tails and they run like a deer."

"Sure—let's settle it," he said.

He moved from the railing. A wicked pleasure spread

over Crane's face. He raised his hands with a practiced lack of show, carrying them low like a man confident of slipping a punch without bothering to block it. Jerry squared off to him.

There was a sudden sharp rap on the railing. The men started. Jerry turned and saw the white helmet of an MP in the shadows down the deck. The MP came on unhurriedly.

"Break it up," he said. "How many wars you guys got to fight before you're happy?"

No one answered him. They were all being very humble. "Anybody ever tell you enlisted men aren't allowed up here?" he asked.

"No, sir," one of the soldiers said.

"Somebody's telling you now. Take off. Don't let me catch you up here again, or you go on report."

They all went down the companionway to the deck below. Crane and his buddies wandered on up the deck. Jerry waited a few minutes. Then he trotted back up the steps and gazed down the deck. There was no one in sight. Taking a deep breath, he headed for the last companionway and hurried up the ladder. It was lighted by dim blue blackout lamps. He came out on a smaller weather deck where space was more constricted. He moved along the rail, trying to decide which door opened on the bridge. It was not so easy as it had been for Sugeta, because blackout curtains were down.

A door opened suddenly, and Jerry pressed into the shadows beside a lifeboat. He had a glimpse of a lighted room where a sailor stood at a wheel. A naval officer stepped onto the deck, closed the door, and walked in the opposite direction from where Jerry was hiding.

After a moment Jerry moved along to the door beyond that of the room the officer had just left. According to Sugeta's description, this should be the navigator's room. But now he had no way of knowing whether the room was occupied or not. He decided to open the door and gamble that it was vacant; if someone was there, he would say, "Excuse me, sir," and depart. Maybe. What was more likely was that he would be called back and questioned. But the thought of going back to admit that he had failed to locate the ship's position caused him suddenly to turn the knob and open the door a few inches.

He gazed into a small, well-lighted room. The walls were painted a glistening gray. There were big map tables about the floor and a cot against one wall. He saw no one in the room. Then his glance was caught by a brass-and-glass instrument lying on one of the tables. A sextant!

Jerry rubbed his damp palms on his trousers and walked inside.

He looked first at a big chart lying on one of the tables. Groups of islands dotted the chart, and there was one big double-island labeled: *New Zealand.* Smaller islands were designated *Samoa, Society Islands, New Caledonia.* His heart racing, he searched a desk for tracing paper. He found some onionskin paper and made tracings so that he could lay them all together and have a complete, large chart. He folded the sheets, tucked them inside his pocket, and picked up the sextant. To his gratification, it had a fluid level, like a surveyor's transit. It was almost a duplicate of the one they had used in astronomy class.

Jerry stepped to the shelf of books and found a nautical almanac. He located a page showing the same constellations he had observed in the sky above the ship. He picked out three bright stars and found them in the table accompanying the star map. Carefully he noted down the figures. He was perspiring and tense, listening for the sound of footfalls on the deck. After he had finished with the almanac, he put it away, wiped his face on his sleeve, and hurried from the navigation room.

Almost at once he heard voices. His intention had been to take sightings immediately and replace the sextant. Now he knew he would not have time to do so. He strode back to the companionway and descended, the sextant under his arm. Suddenly he was panicky and filled with shame. He had no right to be doing this. He had let that stubborn Nisei's pride of his trick him into something he did not actually approve of. But since he had gone this far, he might as well go the rest of the way.

He found a deserted spot and looked up at the stars. He found his stars, shot them, and took readings from the sextant. He fixed the figures in his mind and hurried back to the companionway. Just before he reached it, he saw a man standing inside the stairway. With a shock, he stopped short, staring through the thick tropical darkness.

The man stepped out silently; behind him came another man, and still another. Four men emerged from the companionway, and now Jerry saw that they were Crane and his buddies.

"Take the yellow-bellied so-and-so!" Crane whispered.

They came at Jerry in a rush. Jerry dropped the sextant and jarred his fist against the face of the first man to reach him. The soldier's knees buckled and he sprawled against Jerry. Crane threw a high punch to the side of Jerry's head, stunning him. Jerry found himself on his knees, hurt and dazed. Crane and two other men who were still on their feet seized him by the arms and legs and raised him from the deck.

"Here's one Nip we won't have to worry about!" Crane said viciously. They began carrying him toward the railing. Jerry's whole body stiffened in a spasm of fear. Then he began struggling wildly. The GI's were thrown around by the strength of his thrashing, but they kept their grip on his wrists and ankles. He pulled his legs up and shot them out, hurling two men to their knees. They lumbered up again, swearing but still holding on; he tried to tear his wrists from Crane's grasp, but the soldier hung on. The man Jerry had first knocked down now joined him and took hold of one of Jerry's arms.

Now they were lifting him over the railing. Jerry shouted. Looking down, he saw an oily gleam of water where the bow wave curled away from the ship. Terror seized him. He twisted his wrist in Crane's grasp and was able to get hold of the man's own wrist. Suddenly the men who held his ankles released them and his body swung down into blackness. Yet he managed to hold onto Crane's wrist desperately. He was hanging with his head just at deck-height and his toes kicking against the steel plates of the ship. He cried out again, and heard Crane bawl his own panic; the GI was being pulled over the rail by the weight of Jerry's body. Crane clawed at the hand on his wrist, but Jerry's grip was cemented there by the fear of death.

"Hang onto me!" Crane gasped to his companions. "He's pulling me over!"

Jerry saw them lunge in to seize Crane's arms. Then he heard running footfalls on the deck. He almost wept to see the white helmet of an MP coming out of the darkness. Another man was running up from the other direction.

"As you were!" the MP shouted. "What goes on?"

Two of the men ducked and ran. Crane pleaded to the other, "Hang on, dang you!"

The MP swerved in and reached down to clutch Jerry's free hand. He and Crane hauled him back over the rail; Jerry leaned back against it and then slumped into a sitting posture. His knees had given out. His body was drenched in a cold sweat. He heard the MP talking to Crane.

"What happened here? Did he try to jump overboard?"

"Oh, there was a ruckus. Him and one of the guys that took off were fighting over something. We were wrassling around trying to break it up—"

An officer ran up. Jerry could see a lieutenant colonel's

silver leaves on his shoulders. "What happened, Sergeant?" he asked the MP.

The MP saluted. "I don't know, sir. This man says there was a fight and the other man started to fall overboard. What about that?" he asked Jerry.

Jerry looked up into Crane's sweat-slick, rocky features. "That's right. It was just a friendly tussle," he said weakly.

"Over what?" asked the officer.

"Just—you know, horseplay," Jerry said.

The officer moved to get a better look at him, and as he did so his toe struck the sextant lying near the railing. "What's this?" Jerry's stomach muscles contracted. The officer picked up the instrument and examined it. Then he looked sharply at Crane, his companion, the instrument, and then at Jerry. "This is one of the ship's sextants. Who took this out of the chartroom?"

Jerry stood up, holding to the rail. "Sir, I—I borrowed it."

"For what purpose?"

"I wanted to know where we were. I bet some friends I could find out."

The officer tucked the sextant under his arm. "Who is your superior officer?"

"Lieutenant Bennett is my section chief, sir. I'm in I & R Platoon, Second Battalion."

"Name, rank, and serial number."

Jerry gave him the information, as both he and the

MP wrote it down. "Go to your quarters and remain there," the lieutenant colonel ordered.

"Yes, sir."

"Sergeant," the officer said to the MP, "you'd better escort him. I don't know what went on here, but I've got my own ideas. After you've taken him to his quarters, put a call on the P.A. for all Niseis on the ship to return to quarters and to stay there."

An hour later, Russ came to the cabin where Jerry and the other Niseis were talking over what had happened. Russ looked stern and angry. For the first time, Jerry felt that he and Russ were not merely friends, but officer and enlisted man—on different planes. Russ folded his long frame onto a bunk and gazed at him.

"You meathead," he said.

Jerry lay on his bunk up under the ceiling and gazed wearily at the gray alligator-hide of the paint. The other men, feeling responsible for what had happened, glumly listened in.

I've been talking to Colonel Hunter for the last half-hour," Russ went on. "You know who he is, don't you? Commanding officer of the 5307th. He can make or break anybody in this outfit—including lieutenants whose men get in serious trouble. What was the fight about?" he asked curtly.

"Remember Crane—the man who was giving me a bad time that first morning?"

"Yes."

"I ran into him and some buddies on the way to the bridge tonight. They started to make trouble, but an MP broke it up. When I was coming back they tried to throw me overboard."

"Why didn't you tell the MP that?"

Jerry reached up and scratched a flake of paint from the ceiling. "It seemed like a chance to teach him something about Niseis. Since I didn't report him, he may realize eventually that I saved his neck—after he tried to kill me."

Russ spoke with sour admiration. "I'll give you credit for doing more wrong things in right ways than anybody I've ever known! What about the sextant?"

Sugeta spoke up. He was carving quietly on the stock of his gun. "I needled him into trying to find out where we were."

"That's about what I figured. I'll tell you what Colonel Hunter asked me just now: Do we send Harada back to the States in the brig, or do we give him another chance? In other words—is he disloyal, or isn't he?"

Jerry rose up on an elbow. "They couldn't really think that."

"Not much they couldn't! The security officer was all for sending you back. He figured you were charting one of the patterns our troopships follow, to turn over to the Japanese."

"What did you tell him?"

"What could I tell him? That I didn't know, but I didn't *think* you were. No one really knows but you."

In the thick tropical heat penned against the ceiling, Jerry was sweating. He remembered the last night at Topaz, when his father had quoted to him, "Ye are the light of the world. A city which is set on a hill cannot be hid!" And he closed his eyes with shame.

Russ went on. "Then Hunter said, 'Well, I'll leave it up to you, Lieutenant. Does he go back, or does he go along?' I said that if I lost you, I'd lose one of the best language men in the outfit. I said I'd like to take one more chance on you. He said okay—but it would have to go on your record. That's two strikes on your record, now, Jerry —and three strikes sends you to the bench in any game."

Jerry was too shaken to trust his voice, but he choked, "Thanks."

Russ stood up, lanky, grinning, brown with shipboard tan. "Hunter had a word for me, too. He said, 'I don't set much store by men who lie around getting a tan, Lieutenant. Try to find something to do besides getting your face tanned up.' He's a great guy, but he's got his quirks. But it was no quirk when he said all of you would have to finish the voyage in this stateroom, except for meals and formations."

The men looked at each other, stunned. To spend the rest of the voyage in this cramped and smelly sweatbox! "We'll go nuts!" Sugeta protested.

Russ was looking at the carving on Sugeta's gunstock. "And keep that thing out of sight too, will you? You could be court-martialed for defacing government property. Even though it's a real work of art."

Russ went to the door. He opened it and the night seemed to slip inside like a warm river. As he started out, he looked up at Jerry.

"By the way—just for curiosity—where the heck *are* we?"

Jerry took the copy of the chart from his pocket, made some marks on it, and studied it a moment. "I figure we'll make New Caledonia in the morning," he said.

## CHAPTER 12

# Odd Man Out

Jerry was right. In the morning, the ship made port at Noumea, New Caledonia. Here they picked up 670 emaciated, feverish-looking combat veterans to swell the roster of the unit. In their gaunt faces the men's eyes looked huge and staring. Their skin was yellow with atabrine—the antimalarial pill. Jerry watched them with awe as they boarded ship. These men had seen combat—the death and terror of the battlefield. Yet they had had the courage to volunteer for hazardous service. Jerry wondered, with a coolness in his blood, whether he would find the same kind of courage in himself. The closer a man got to combat, it seemed, the more he questioned his courage.

The transport sailed again, putting in a few days later at Brisbane, Australia, where three hundred more veterans of the war-swept, bloody islands boarded. The roster was now complete; 5307th Composite Unit (Provisional) was at full strength.

Again the ship headed into the open sea. This time the course was due south. The weather grew colder as she steamed below the equator, making for the southeastern tip of Australia. Having passed it, the transport headed west across the flat underside of the continent. The gray seas roughened, and rain squalls lashed the decks. SF 1280 cleared the far western horn of land. She swung north again, putting in finally on the west coast of Australia at the small port of Fremantle, near Perth. They glimpsed submarine pens where low, sinister silhouettes were visible. Here the ship took on supplies with that same grim haste which characterized every movement of the ship's crew, in contrast to the dead languor of the troops. Then she ran out again, silent and hurried.

As she turned north, the feeling grew that they were approaching the end of the voyage. Over thirty days had passed, and in their hot and stuffy quarters the Niseis bickered, polished shoes and brass, and invented games to try to keep from going mad with boredom.

Pamphlets were issued one day explaining a new type of combat unit known as a Long Range Penetration Group. L.R.P.G.'s, the booklet explained, had the task of getting behind the enemy lines and causing all possible havoc—disrupting communications, setting ambuscades to trap the enemy's patrols, keeping him off balance with swift, bloody stabs at his weakest points.

In typical Army fashion, however, no one bothered to explain whether the 5307th was an L.R.P.G. or not.

At last one night orders came over the public address system to pack all gear immediately—they would make port at Bombay, India, in the morning.

Mystery and excitement charged the whole ship. It was

not difficult to deduce where the 5307th was going to do her fighting. The Japanese had overrun Burma and were forging west into India. Somewhere along the Indian-Burmese border, probably, they would cross into the Burmese jungles to make their attempt at long-range harassment of the enemy.

The goal of such a campaign against the Japanese in Burma was to reopen the Burma Road—the only road across the Himalayas into China. It was of critical importance to keep China supplied in her fight against the Japanese on her home soil, but with the Japanese occupying Burma, those supplies had to be flown across Burma and over the towering Himalayas before they reached the Chinese troops. Every month saw the toll of lost cargo planes mount. So it was plain that Allied headquarters had at last decided to attempt the recovery of Burma, and thus move supplies by truck from India across Burma, and over the Burma Road into China, in order to step up the pace of the war on that front.

In the hot, sticky morning, they marched down the gangplank at Bombay and crossed a dock thronged with porters and beggars. Jerry stumbled as he tried to anticipate the roll of a deck which was no longer rolling. With fascination and an involuntary shudder, he looked at the filthy, turbaned porters and beggars, their skinny limbs jointed like plumbing.

In long files, the soldiers marched under heavy barracks bags to a line of old wooden railroad coaches waiting for them on a siding. They took seats in a filth of trash and cockroaches, among odors of wood smoke and exotic food smells. The train clattered from the city.

A few hours later it halted near a tiny plains town. As the red dust swirled about them, the three thousand men marched to a dreary tent city set up to accommodate them. After the intense blue of the ocean, this white-and-terra-cotta world was depressing. They spent two days settling in. Then the training started. It was hard and punishing work. Long toughening marches took the combat teams out across the plaster-dry plains to a wilderness of bare, broken hills which resembled the rubble of a giant brickyard. They ran bayonet courses, practiced compass-reading, crawled under barbed wire with live ammunition stinging the air above them. Every muscle in Jerry's body was tender.

Suddenly the regiment was moving again.

Packs were rolled and the outfit marched back to the railroad siding. In creaking wooden coaches which lurched over the plains like camels, they traveled east for three days. The country changed, the hills grew rougher, the gullies deepened. Tough bushes and trees gave the land a deceptively green and woolly look, but when at last they detrained and set out across it, they learned that every branch was armed with poisonous thorns. They marched through this thorn-scrub and tangled woods to the Betwa River. Islands of tent towns dotted the broad green plain, and not far east rose a high range of hills clad with jungle.

And now at last, before final training began, they were told why they were in India.

The 5307th Composite Unit was part of a larger group called "Galahad Force," the sword and sinew of "Operation Galahad," which, the men now learned, was the designation of a bold attempt to drive the Japanese out of Burma and reopen the Burma Road to China.

It would be commanded by the British Brigadier Wingate, and would consist of three main combat groups: the Americans, the British, and a Chinese expeditionary force. Most of the British troops would be fierce Indian Ghurkas. Members of the Hindu sect, the Ghurkas were big men whose entire mission in life was fighting. They did not even stoop to doing their own cooking or cleaning-up of their camps: members of an inferior Indian caste followed them wherever they fought, to do these chores.

The plan was for a Chinese force to swarm out of China into northeast Burma, just as the Americans, aided by the Chinese Expeditionary Force, pushed in from India. British air commandos, dropped by parachute and glider, would smash at the Japanese at other points. Thus the Japanese army in Burma would be squeezed in a three-jawed vise. If they could be forced down into southern Burma, the Burma Road could be reopened. But all that really interested the Americans was the news that they would shortly be marching into the Burmese jungle in an attempt to get around behind the Japanese force on the Burmese border.

American and Chinese troops, they were told, would be under the command of General Joseph W. "Vinegar Joe" Stilwell. However, General Frank D. Merrill would lead them into combat.

A newsman looked at the tough jungle fighters one day and said to Merrill, "They look more like marauders than soldiers!" In his news stories he began referring to the Americans in Galahad Force as "Merrill's Marauders." The name had a flavor of freebootery which they liked, and the name stuck.

Final training was an exercise in exhaustion. If they had not understood it before, they realized now that they were being taught the art of killing. They practiced attacks upon entrenchments, pillboxes and roadblocks; they set booby traps and studied the demolition of bridges and fortifications. They waded rivers at night and practiced taking air-drops of supplies, for once they entered Burma all their supplies would have to be flown into the jungle and parachuted to them.

The language men were split up, four being assigned to each battalion. They trained with the Intelligence and Reconnaissance platoons, the eyes and ears of the Army. In combat, their mission would be to range far ahead of the main column, search out the enemy, and test his strength. Since the I & R platoons would run the greatest risks, their training was the hardest. Jerry was numb with fatigue; he never caught up on sleep or had enough to eat. Some of the tactical problems took them into the thorn-jungle for three days at a time. They slept in breaks of two or three hours, then clambered up and went on through the thickets at double time.

But somehow their mail followed them; and that thin thread leading back to home and family made the frustrations of training less critical for a while. A little L-plane would dip from the brassy Indian sky and bags of mail would come parachuting down. The cry of "Mail Call!" would be heard all over camp that night. Jerry learned from his letters that his father had been made foreman of his work gang, that Helen was interested in a boy who wanted to be a doctor when the war was over, that his mother was unable to get guitar strings for the little samisen she used to play and sing to, that Sam was first baseman on a camp baseball team. He sighed. He felt somehow left out. Probably they felt the same way—that they had been hung high on a limb for the duration of the war. But at least they were together, while he was out here in a wild, thorny land with the loneliest, most hazardous work in the world ahead of him.

Once, the platoon had a field problem with the British and Indian troops. Afterward they had a few minutes to talk with them and trade food rations. The Indian troops were big, dark-skinned native soldiers who carried long *kukris*—knives like the curved blades of pruning hooks. Jerry asked a Ghurka to show him his knife. The soldier drew the long knife, slashed a small cut in his finger with the razor-edge of it, and exhibited the knife. Jerry stared at the blood on the man's finger. The Ghurka's white grin flashed.

"A Ghurka must never draw his knife without giving it blood to drink," he explained.

Jerry was sorry he had asked to see the knife. He never asked again, after learning that there was a superstition against baring a knife without letting it taste blood.

One day there was an exercise which took them into some craggy hills. They practiced moving down a narrow aisle through the brush and being fired on by an enemy trailblock—three machine guns set up in the deadly Japanese S-pattern. After the exercise the I & R platoon assembled on a hilltop from which they could see the ancient country running out into heat haze on all sides. In the east could be discerned mountains cloaked with jungle—the mountains into which they would march some day soon.

They slipped their pack straps and lay on the ground, exhausted. Jerry stared up into the clear, hot sky through branches of a thorn tree, watching three vultures circle silently on the rim of an invisible wheel. Russ took a sip of chlorinated water from his canteen and lay back.

"If I had it all to do over again," he said, "I'd put in for a job managing a PX."

"Fine, patriotic soldier you are," muttered Jerry.

"Did you hear that a captain was carried off by mosquitos last night?"

"No, but I hope it was the one who marched us in at double-time."

Russ was quiet a moment. "I wonder what combat will really be like . . . I mean, what's it like to have somebody lying out there firing *at* you—not just seeing how close he can come without hitting you? Somebody actually being paid to kill you! Sure, we've crawled under live firing and had pig's blood dumped on us so we can see how we'd look wounded. But what will it *really* be like?"

It was a question that was probably old in Genghis Khan's time. "I figure it'll be like training, only with bullets," Jerry said.

From a little distance away, where he lay in the latticed shade of a leafless tree, one of the other I & R men chuckled. He was one of the platoon's combat veterans.

"Sonny, this is a picnic!" he drawled. "You haven't got malaria and dysentery, and mortar shells dropping on you like coconuts. You haven't even slept in a foxhole half-full of water with no food for two days. This is the best deal I've had since I shipped out of Seattle."

"You must have had some rough ones, then. Where were you before you came here?"

"New Guinea. Guadalcanal . . ." The soldier's gaunt face seemed to brood, as though the names dug up half-buried memories.

"Why did you volunteer for the Marauders?" Jerry asked him.

The soldier grinned. "I got myself in a little trouble. Found a bottle of rice wine the Japs left behind and got drunk on it. One thing led to another, and they gave me a choice of volunteering or doing six months at hard labor."

"What do you think this mission's going to be like?" Russ asked him.

"Can't say. This long-range-penetration stuff is too new. I know the Japs tore the devil out of Wingate when he tried it last year. What gets me is the idea of all supply being by air. What if we get socked in by rain and fog? How do they supply us then? And there's no law says a jungle can't be so dense we can't put up an aerial to tell them where to drop the food!"

"Speaking of planes . . ." Russ pointed toward the east. A little L-4 plane, looking like a small *Spirit of St. Louis,* was flying up from the southeast. They could hear its motor throbbing in the hot air. It dipped down toward the battalion's landing strip on the plain.

"Oh-oh!" the veteran exclaimed. "Somebody's dyin'. You've got to be dyin' to get flown out of *this* brier patch. Else some chicken colonel's flying in to chew us out."

That afternoon an Air Force sergeant was waiting before the headquarters tent when they shambled in. He seemed to be looking for the Niseis, for he straightened up and signaled to Jerry when he saw them passing on the way to the company area. He was a stubby, sleepy-looking man wearing suntans and a baseball cap, all quite clean. His face was square, hard, and with narrow blue eyes. He wore an unlighted cigarette over one ear.

"Which one's Lieutenant Bennett, soldier?" he asked.

"I'm Bennett," Russ told him.

"Your platoon leader said to give you this," the sergeant said. He handed Russ an envelope. Russ opened it, read it to himself, and then read it aloud.

"*You will immediately, repeat, immediately, select one member ATIS group for temporary duty combat area. This man to be expert linguist. Said enlisted man will be carried on detached duty with OSS 101 Detachment. Transportation is provided herewith.*"

Russ looked up. " 'Transportation' meaning the plane you flew in?"

"That's right. Pick your man, Lieutenant. They're mighty itchy for a linguist back there in the jungle." The sergeant lighted his cigarette and snapped the match in two.

"The jungle!" Russ said. "I didn't know we had any units in combat yet."

"We don't. This is just a bunch of Kachin tribesmen under an American officer. They're called Kachin Rangers. They're a hit-and-run outfit, but they do their share of damage."

"Why do they need a translator?"

"They captured a Jap pilot yesterday. He crashed his Zero in a rice paddy and they took him alive. At least he was still alive when I left. Headquarters wants somebody to work him over."

Russ scratched his chin. "How long will this take?"

"Maybe two days. We can make Ledo or Margherita

before dark. In the morning we'll land in the Hukawng Valley, where the unit's bivouacked. As soon as your man's questioned the prisoner, I'll fly him out again."

Russ looked around. Every dusty face was alert. Jerry had a keen desire to be chosen, yet under his excitement ran a dark strain of realism. Obviously the Kachins were deep in enemy territory, where capture was a strong possibility. And capture was the special nightmare of the Nisei.

"Let's see hands for Burma," Russ said quietly.

Jerry, Sugeta, and Matsumoto raised their hands. "That's what I thought," Russ said. He pulled three coins from his pocket and handed one to each. "Odd man goes."

They flipped the coins and smacked them onto the backs of their hands. Matsumoto and Sugeta had thrown tails; Jerry had thrown heads. Jerry felt a goose-fleshy thrill. The Air Force man dropped the broken match and trampled it in the dust.

"Let's go, Odd Man!" he said. "Time's wasting. You'd better draw some ten-in-one rations. Where we're going, they're living on bamboo sprouts."

Jerry got some rations, made a light pack of a few essentials, and hurried back to the section tent. The flier was now waiting in a jeep driven by Russ. Ben and Matsumoto were standing beside it.

"Some guys have all the luck," Ben complained as Jerry climbed in.

"Ain't it the truth?" agreed the flier. "The only question is, who's the lucky one—you or Odd Man?"

The jeep rolled off in a cloud of cinnamon-colored dust. At the landing strip, Jerry tossed his pack into the cabin of the L-4 plane while the flier warmed up the engine. Russ offered his hand, a little embarrassed to appear formal, yet obviously feeling that it might be a longer trip Jerry was leaving on than anyone could foresee.

"Get back to us soon," he shouted over the engine's roar.

"Two days!" Jerry promised.

But as he settled into the bucket seat, he wondered, *Two days—or never?* For the end of the show might come for him, or for all of them, before he came back.

CHAPTER 13

# Deserted Village

At dusk the plane dropped from the clouds to circle above the high mountains of the Burmese-Indian border. Jerry peered down at what looked like a rich green carpet thrown over the jagged backbones of mountain ranges and the basins of broad, many-rivered valleys. Directly below the plane, the fabric of the jungle had been torn open to reveal a raw, red pattern of fields, roads, and supply dumps. Out of this jumble of raw earth a road went backing and switching down through the deep mountain canyons to the valleys of northern Burma.

The pilot tapped Jerry's knee. "That's Margherita!" he shouted over the flapping roar of the engine. "The road is the Ledo Road—biggest road-building job in history, next to the Burma Road! You and your buddies will be walking down it one of these days. . . ."

With the ease of a bird, the little L-4 plane dipped down to a runway and ran to the edge of the landing field. In the dusk, Jerry glimpsed scores of trucks, graders, and vehicles of nearly every kind. Little clusters of native *bashas* were visible—huts on stilts, with palm-thatched roofs. Great clouds of dust were sucked up from the roads by the roaring trucks.

They slept that night in a *basha* on the edge of the dripping rain forest. ("And this is the dry season!" the flier said.) Through open doors in the split-bamboo walls stole the faintly acrid breath of the nearby jungle, damp and foreign-smelling, and as Jerry lay inhaling it he shivered suddenly, both from the dampness and from excitement. There swept over him a disturbing feeling of being ill-prepared for his job. The shocking thought that he might freeze up completely chilled him. What if he became too scared to remember the recently learned military words the man might use? Or worse, what if the man spoke in a soldier jargon that made no sense? Before dawn, the Air Force sergeant shook Jerry awake.

"Hit the deck, Odd Man," he said.

Taking off, they circled the great staging area of Margherita, where the pilot said the Marauders would assemble before commencing their long march down the Ledo Road. As they headed southeast, the beauty of the country spread below them—the green mountain ranges and the valleys where rivers twisted through a thousand turns, glittering like ice. In the distance everything was blue with morning haze. Directly ahead Jerry discerned a few curls of smoke rising into the air. The sergeant saw him looking at them.

"Jap bivouacs!" he shouted.

Jerry shivered. They were now definitely behind the enemy's lines.

In a surprisingly short time they were dropping down again. A couple of clearings were discernible where thatched *bashas* grouped themselves in tiny villages, each village flanked by its own rice paddies where Karen and Kachin tribesmen grew their provisions.

The pilot pointed. "See the landing strip?"

Jerry saw a river, a fairly large one moving with hairpin turnings toward the south. Two villages could be seen in the jungle, one of them quite close and with smoky fires visible. But he could not make out a landing strip.

"You haven't got your air-eyes yet," the pilot commented. "That village—see it? It's deserted. The rice paddies are dry. We're going to land on one of them—you can see my tracks from yesterday. That's where the Jap pilot was trying to land when he cracked up. This baby just loves rice paddies. A Zero is too hot for a rough field. The pilot wouldn't have tried to land there if he hadn't been in trouble. Here we go!" he said.

The floor of the jungle rocked suddenly like a disk on a pivot. It swerved up, swung around so that northbound rivers were running south, leveled itself, and the plane's engine cut down to a popping idle. They were heading sharply down into the paddies, which resembled graham crackers separated by low dikes of earth. The jungle crowded in on them on three sides, the village bounded them on the fourth. The trees were very tall and slender, many of them draped with vines. Jerry searched for signs of life—smoke, dust, or clothing hung on branches, but saw nothing but a wrecked plane at one end of the paddies. Somehow the aching silence and utter strangeness of the whole scene made him think of home—of chopping weeds in summer; his mother bringing sandwiches to them when they were too busy to take time off to come in; of the delicious languor of lying in the sand at the beach, drenched in sunlight—

The plane touched down, bounced, and rolled to a stop.

From the jungle trotted a file of small brown-skinned men in green shirts and shorts. They wore hats like the Australian soldiers'—wide-brimmed and pinned up rakishly on one side—and all carried weapons. As they moved upon the plane, Jerry felt his mouth go dry.

"Are these our people?" he asked nervously.

"I wouldn't be sitting here if they weren't. That's Chet Khin in the lead—Captain Cork's number one boy. He calls him Chicken—that's the way his name reads in English."

"They look like Boy Scouts!" Jerry commented.

"They aren't. At least they're not helping any Japs across the street this season!"

He had brought a few small crates of supplies from Margherita, and while Jerry jumped down and slung his field pack over one shoulder, he began dragging crates forward and handing them down to the Kachins. The men crowded about Jerry, smiling disarmingly. At first glance he liked them. Many of them were only twelve or thirteen years old. They were not sly and suspicious-looking like the impoverished people of India. They looked friendly, alert, and healthy. They had fine features, and their big smiles seemed to say, in any language, "Friend!"

One of them moved close to Jerry. He was about twenty years old, perhaps five feet five inches tall, and carried a burp gun slung around his neck. "Esscuse," he said to Jerry, reaching up to lift his plastic helmet liner. Jerry had slung his helmet on his pack. He looked at Jerry's close-cropped hair, nodded approvingly, and let the hat drop back.

Jerry asked the sergeant, "What was that for?"

"Just a precaution," the flier said. "You'll get used to it. You see, the Japs all shave their heads. No hair—Jap; hair—Nisei."

Jerry's training had not mentioned this custom of the Japanese troops. "Why do they shave their heads?" he asked.

"Head lice. There's every kind of louse known to man in these hills. Shave the head—no head lice. We get the same result with DDT."

A strangely clad figure in a khaki shirt and blue trousers cut off below the knees emerged from the jungle, carrying a carbine. He sauntered toward the plane, eating a field-ration candy bar. He wore a flat World War I-style helmet, and his canvas-and-rubber jungle boots came well above his ankles. The strangest thing about him was a thick black beard, about an inch long so that it stood straight out like a shoebrush.

Seeing his captain's bars, Jerry saluted. The officer returned the salute casually.

"Private Harada reporting, sir," Jerry said.

"I'm Captain Cork. We're glad to see you. You got here just in time—in an hour or so we've got to move. Apparently the Japs spotted the plane yesterday and the boys say they've got a patrol coming after us." He said this in the most offhand manner imaginable, as though he might have been announcing the possibility of rain.

"Of course we'd have left a signal fire to flag you off," he added. "Come on and have a look at our prisoner. He's only the second one we ever took. I hope he'll talk before we move out, because he probably won't survive the jolting around."

Jerry expected to be taken into the village. But Captain Cork walked toward the bamboo thicket at the far end of the paddy field. "Aren't you bivouacked in the village?" Jerry asked.

"Oh, no—we never bivouac in a village. The fires are just to force the enemy to investigate to make sure we aren't there—while we take off."

A very narrow trail was hacked into the prickly bamboo. The growth was so dense that the bamboo had to be cut off at ground level and again six feet above the ground. The interlaced top-growth would not permit the cut spears to fall. The severed sections were pulled out, and a trail like a tunnel resulted. The bamboo thicket ended and they were in a forest of slender trees which went up twenty or thirty feet to the first branches. Below was a dense growth of vines, creepers, and palmlike plants rooted in a loamy earth redolent of decaying vegetation. The brush had been hacked back on either side to make room for a bivouac area. A few crates of supplies lay about among empty tin cans and carrying-poles with baskets at either end.

On a tarp at the base of a tree lay the prisoner.

The Kachin who was guarding him rose and said something to Captain Cork in the Jingpaw dialect.

Cork said to Jerry, "He says he's been talking quite a bit—feverish, I expect. I hope he's not too far gone to cooperate if he wants to."

Jerry squatted beside the man. He had brought cigarettes with him for the prisoner—a helpful device, the training manual said. The man's face was very sallow, indicating loss of blood. His flying jacket was open, torn down one side and stiff with dried blood. His shirt had been opened and there was a glimpse of blood-soaked bandages underneath. On the ground near him lay three small books and some old letters.

"We found these on him," Cork said quietly. "Damn. He looks as though he's in bad shape."

Jerry felt a sudden, unexpected sympathy for the man. Though he was the enemy, and had probably machine-gunned civilians in the streets of Rangoon and Mandalay during the invasion, still he was a human being in trouble, and it was impossible not to feel a twinge of pity for him.

"*Tabako o dozo?*" Jerry asked softly.

The narrow eyes opened quickly and the man smiled at Jerry with joyful surprise—but then looked past Jerry and saw the familiar Caucasian features of Captain Cork, and the green-clad Kachin Rangers standing about. He closed his eyes with a grimace. It had been a cruel but unintentional joke—to permit him to think he had somehow been rescued by his own countrymen, and then let him learn he was still a prisoner.

"*Arigato,*" he muttered, moving one hand slightly.

Jerry opened the small two-cigarette pack and put one of the cigarettes in the man's lips. He struck a match and helped him light the cigarette. "What is your name?" he asked him.

"Hiroshi Sato."

"What is your unit?"

A fly landed on the man's cheek. He frowned but lacked strength to brush it off. Jerry brushed it away. "I do not wish to say," the prisoner murmured.

"Where are you based?" Jerry asked.

"I do not wish to say."

"Who is your commanding officer?"

Sato shook his head feebly. Jerry glanced up at Captain Cork with a shrug. "He's not very talkative. . . . How many planes are there in your unit?" he asked the prisoner.

Blowing smoke around the cigarette, the man replied, "It is not required of me to tell you."

An angry frustration nettled Jerry. He was suddenly

conscious of the heat—damp and clinging, like steam. "Wouldn't you like your jacket off?" he asked.

"Yes. Please."

Jerry started to remove it, but it pained the man so that he groaned and his face turned white. Chet Khin drew a knife and knelt beside the prisoner. He cut the sleeves neatly from his jacket and Jerry and Cork drew them off. Then he slashed a cut from each sleeve hole to the zipper and the jacket fell off. Beneath it was a short-sleeved white shirt, sodden with blood on one side and with a bandage showing beneath.

"I'm not getting anywhere," Jerry told Captain Cork.

Cork rubbed his whiskery jaw. "What we especially want to get out of him is this: What about Lieutenant Shinoda? He's their top pilot in the CBI. Where is he? Is he still alive? What's his unit? Ask him."

"*Shinoda-san wa doko desu ka?*" Jerry asked.

The prisoner smiled faintly. "Who is Shinoda? I have never heard of him."

Jerry sat back. "No luck."

A Ranger came trotting into the bivouac area from the rice paddies. He spoke rapidly to Cork, who rose in disgust.

"They're only a couple of miles off—a forty- or fifty-man patrol. If we didn't have this prisoner on our hands, we'd set up a trailblock and knock off a few of them."

"What about the plane?" Jerry asked.

"The pilot's getting ready to take off right now. We'll

either find a new strip and radio him when he cruises over, or try to come back here after the patrol's left. Keep working on this man—I've got to get my boys moving."

One of the Kachins brought cooked rice in a trough-like plate—a foot-long section of bamboo with the top cut out of it. Jerry offered the flier some rice, but the man shook his head. He himself ate, asking the man a question from time to time. He picked up the books and letters and looked them over. One of the books was a diary, with entries written in very small *sosho*. There might be valuable information in this, and Jerry tucked it away in his pocket. The other book was a volume of Japanese poetry. The letters were from the pilot's wife and parents, pathetic in their concern over him and in their attempt to minimize the effects of the war on their home city.

During this, the Kachins had been swiftly breaking camp. Two men came with a litter improvised of bamboo and vines and moved the prisoner onto it.

"Where are we going?" the prisoner asked Jerry.

"We're moving to a new bivouac."

Half the patrol had already moved out. They heard the roar of the L-plane winging away. Cork spoke to the Kachins, who picked up the litter and swung into the line of march. There were about thirty Rangers and the prisoner was to travel at the middle of the column.

"Okay," the big bearded man told Jerry. "Stay with him. Some of these people get full of talk just before they die. Try to convince him Japan's going to lose anyway, and he might as well hurry the process by helping us."

Jerry voiced something that had been in his mind for an hour. "How are we going to keep ahead of the Jap patrol with this man to slow us down?"

"He won't slow us down—my boys move as fast loaded as unloaded. Also I'm leaving Chicken and two men to start fires in the bush and make them investigate. Then they'll toss a few grenades and take off."

As they headed down the trail, there was a prickly feeling of hairs rising on the back of Jerry's neck. He felt utterly incompetent and bewildered. If a machine gun should open up on us, he thought, I'd forget everything I've been told to do! He felt absolutely certain that he would be paralyzed with fright.

CHAPTER 14

# "To Die for Nippon!"

They came to the bank of a clear, cold stream. The water was only about two feet deep, flowing brilliantly over colored pebbles. Though the sun was directly overhead, no direct rays struck the water. The light as it descended through the leaves made the very air seem tinged with green. The heat, the gnats, and the mosquitoes were troublesome.

There was a delay while the Kachins crossed. Jerry knelt by the prisoner, who had been lowered to the ground while the river-crossing started. He saw that the man was shivering with fever.

"Wouldn't you like a drink?" he asked.

"Please. If it is no trouble."

Jerry brought water in one of the Kachin's bamboo cups. The Japanese drank thirstily, looking up at Jerry, then lay back and closed his eyes.

"You are from Kyushu," Jerry said.

"How did you know?"

"I read your letters."

The pilot's mouth twitched. Then as though repeating something he had read, he murmured, "It is good to die for our divine Nippon."

"It is better to live," Jerry said.

"But I am going to die," the prisoner said, "and that is good, too."

"Do you like poetry?" Jerry asked him.

"Yes. I have written some poetry."

"I'd like to read some of it."

"It isn't here."

"Would you like me to read to you from your book of poems?"

"It doesn't matter. . . . Yes, please do," the prisoner said suddenly.

Jerry opened the book carefully, hoping it would break open at a much-read page. Apparently it did so, for there was a tiny check mark beside a poem on one page. It was a *haiku,* one of the three-line poems the Japanese loved to read and write, delicate thoughts imprisoned in a few words, like butterflies' wings under glass. He read softly:

"*Refreshingly*
*After the violent storm*
*The moon rose radiant,*"

Sato smiled to himself.

Then he began to murmur something, and Jerry leaned close to hear.

"*In blossom today, then scattered;*
*Life is so like a delicate flower.*
*How can one expect the fragrance to last forever?*"

"That's beautiful," Jerry said. "Did you write it yourself?"

"One of our finest admirals wrote it—Ohnishi."

Just then the Kachins unceremoniously picked up the litter, and Sato moaned softly. While he was carried across the stream, Chicken and the other two Rangers trotted up to Captain Cork, who stood at the river crossing. They talked, laughing, and Cork smiled.

"Good hunting!" the captain told Jerry. "They got four sure kills and a couple of probables. They think the Japs have pulled back to the village until they know what they're up against. One of our men has stayed to keep an eye on them. That's the nice thing about jungle war—the enemy never knows whether there are three of you or three hundred. The fighting's done on the trails and only a few men can get into action at a time. How are you making out with the prisoner?"

"He's getting pretty weak," Jerry said gloomily.

The patrol marched another two miles and halted. Captain Cork posted sentries and sent out a couple of two-man patrols to scout the area.

Jerry took some more water to the prisoner. "Is Lieutenant Shinoda in your outfit?" he asked him.

The prisoner did not reply.

"Our commanding officer says he's your top pilot—a very brave man."

The black, slanted eyes opened. "He is courageous and skillful, he has a tiger in his heart!"

"Not the kind of man to like poetry, I suppose," Jerry said.

"He wrote poetry as beautifully as he flew a plane. He did everything well. . . ."

Suddenly Jerry leaned forward. "You say he *did* everything well. Is he dead?"

Sato frowned, realizing he had given something away. "No. He is not dead."

"Sato-san," Jerry said earnestly, "don't you know that thousands of men like Shinoda must die every week the war continues? And for what good? Japan has lost ground every day since she lost Guadalcanal. Her navy is being completely destroyed. The equipment she gives her fighting men is growing poorer. The pilot who flew me in here said your own plane was inferior to the Zeroes you were flying a year ago. Why not help us end the war and save Japan from complete ruin?"

The prisoner looked out dully from his sad, feverish eyes. He began to whisper. "The planes are like toys! So fragile! It is like riding a moth to fly a Zero."

Jerry glanced quickly at Captain Cork and gave a slight nod. Cork made the V-sign with his fingers.

"Did Shinoda crack up in one of them?" Jerry asked.

"No. He is in Japan."

"In Japan! Why?"

"For the defense of the home islands, in case there are more air raids. All our best pilots are being called in for the defense of our divine Nippon. Shinoda left three months ago."

"How many fliers are left in Burma?"

"As many as before—but boys, hardly trained at all, and flying planes as flimsy as kites! It is cruel. They fly out to attack warships—but they seldom come back."

"What is your unit, Sato-san?" Jerry asked. He held his breath.

After a moment Sato spoke feebly. "I am with the Eleventh Special Air Unit. Our base is at Rail Indaw, Burma."

He explained the unit's table of organization in detail. Then he stopped speaking, exhausted and shaking with fever. "To die so far from one's homeland!" he whispered.

"I will write your family if I am able," Jerry said. "But you may see them again yourself."

He moved away a few feet and sat on the ground to write in his notebook everything the man had said. When he had finished, he handed it to Cork.

"Good boy!" Cork commended. "I'll encode this and try to radio it out today. Though our radio is only good for about twenty miles. But one of our fliers might pick it up."

A few hours later the flier died. Cork had him buried beside the trail. To Jerry, there was something terribly sad about that grave hidden in the jungle. For this man, who had loved his family and his country, and wrote poetry, was now only a number erased from a blackboard. Any meaning he might have had for mankind, any contribution he might have made, was forever washed out.

"I like the ugly ones better," Captain Cork said softly behind Jerry. "The infantrymen who scream at us. They don't start you thinking."

A warm, tingling darkness descended. High overhead, monkeys could be heard chattering; a fever-bird made its startling four-note cry. A huge moth fluttered against Jerry's face and he slapped at it in queasy panic. Two Kachins came in with the information that the Japanese patrol had bivouacked in the village. They had posted sentries for the night. Apparently they had orders not to range beyond a certain distance, or else they were uncertain what force they were up against.

"We'd better do something about that gang," Cork said. "Maybe we can take us a prisoner—at least kill a few of the blighters. I'll take about fifteen boys and leave the rest here."

"What about me?" Jerry asked. "Do you want me to go along?"

Scratching his beard, the captain gazed at him seriously. "I'm not *asking* you to come," he said. "You've already accomplished your mission. But you might be able to make yourself right useful, if you're willing."

Jerry picked up his carbine and was surprised to find his palms slippery with sweat. "Let's go!"

## CHAPTER 15

# Blood Bath

Near the village, Captain Cork led the patrol from the main trail. The darkness was so great, the air so thick with steamy jungle odors, that Jerry felt suffocated. Cork whispered to him that they were now nearing the rice paddies where the plane had landed that morning.

"Stick close. There's a trail here, but you can't see it. We usually stay on the main trails, since a patrol going through the jungle makes more noise than a herd of water buffalo. But this close to the village they'll have the trails ambuscaded."

This was Kachin country, and the little warriors knew every track in the jungle. Suddenly they stopped on the very edge of the rice paddies. In the distance, a fire could be seen in the village. Cork pressed down on Jerry's shoulder and he sank to the ground. A few men went out to scout the perimeter of the village. Jerry lay there on the soft earth, peering across the flat fields toward the *bashas* where cook-fires were blazing. He could see several of the stilted huts plainly. He kept swallowing, but his mouth was as dry as plaster; he wished he had some of the Army's ghastly lemon drops to keep it moist.

The Rangers came back to report no sentries close to the village. "We're already inside their perimeter!" Cork said with a wry grin. "A boy's gone in to count them and see what kind of weapons they've got."

Jerry felt his stomach cramp with fear. A large, disgraceful terror was shaking him like a fever. He felt somehow tricked. The Army told you all about it—except the fear. They didn't explain what to do when you felt like running—when all you could think of was that you were not only behind the lines, but *inside their perimeter—their own sentry line!* And what about the fact that a Nisei was sure to be tortured if he was captured? He was ashamed of his fear, but it lay inside him as real and debilitating as a terrible stomach-ache. As frightened as he was, one thing stood out clearly in his mind: Cork and the Kachins would base their opinions of all Niseis on how this one Nisei, of all the thousands in the country, stood up under fire.

"Been in combat before?" Captain Cork asked mildly.

"No, sir."

"Well, it's not so bad after the first big shock wears off. There's that horrible noise!—and maybe the man next to you screams, and there's blood all over both of you. You see? Well, your mind pulls a curtain after a while, and you do your duty and the devil with the rest. The worst part is *fearing* the action—not the action itself."

Ashamed of his fears, Jerry found himself shaking.

Small fire-lit figures came and went in the village. Then the villagers seemed to settle down to their evening meal.

"What's that?" Jerry asked suddenly. He had heard singing.

"Oh, they're always singing," the captain whispered. "They've got these do-or-die battalion songs they roar at each other—or so I've heard. They might be the Japanese version of 'Lili Marlene,' for all I know."

An idea came to Jerry which almost made him sick with fright. Lying there, he watched the Kachins move out across the paddies to the village. He rested his chin on the stock of his carbine, afraid to voice his thoughts.

"I wonder if that bunch is attached to Tanaka's Eighteenth Division," Cork mused.

"Who's he?" Jerry asked, feeling very inadequately prepared.

"The hero of Singapore—quite a military man. He pulled a 'Marching Through Georgia' out here—only he marched from Singapore, through the Malay States, and across Burma. One of my jobs is to keep an eye out for any new divisions the Japs throw into the fight—so we'll know what we're up against."

"Would it help," Jerry asked, "if you knew what battalion the patrol is attached to?"

Cork looked at Jerry in the darkness. "That's a thought, now! You bet it would." Jerry sensed, somehow, that the officer had maneuvered things so that he would make the suggestion himself. "If I knew their battalion, I could probably figure out their regiment and division. You bet it would help!"

Jerry's tongue stuck to the roof of his mouth. "I—I'll crawl up and see if I can understand what they're singing, then."

"Good boy! I heard you Niseis were mighty gutty customers. Wait'll the boys get back. Then you can take off with a guide."

The Kachins returned to report that there were probably seventy-five men in the patrol; that they had knee-mortars, lightweight Nambu machine guns, a couple of heavies, and even a pack howitzer.

Cork snorted. "Ostentatious display of strength," he declared. He put his hand on Jerry's back. "Chicken will take a few boys over there now and raise a little hell, after you've done your translation. Sure you want in on it?"

Jerry nodded, mechanically rising to his feet. He fed a shell into the carbine and waited while Chet Khin gathered six of the Rangers. All of them carried burp guns and grenades. It was incongruous to see such lethal weapons in the hands of mere boys.

"Out you go," Captain Cork ordered.

Behind Chet Khin, Jerry and the others strung off across the neglected rice paddy in a darkness so great they could hardly see their feet. It was like floating. Climbing over one of the low dikes, they moved across the second paddy, the village coming closer now and the singing becoming much louder. Jerry halted to listen. He could catch a few words only. The distance was still too great. Chet Khin went forward again. The fire and the huts were only thirty yards away. The Kachin dropped to his knees and began to crawl. Jerry took his cue and crawled behind him.

Now they were in some small shrubs just short of the *bashas.* The fire was in the lane between two rows of huts, so close that Jerry could see the little bronze stars gleaming dully on the soldiers' caps as they passed stone bottles of rice wine. He could make out their features, thin and undernourished but keen. The veterans of Singapore—or another group? He had heard stories of the cruelty of the Japanese at Singapore, machine-gunning British nurses and civilians, slaughtering their prisoners by the hundred.

Suddenly, quite plainly, he could understand the words of the song.

*"Though my body decay in Guadalcanal,*
*My spirit will persist in defense of the homeland."*

He nodded enthusiastically to Chet Khin, who grinned. The Kachin whispered to his companions. They began creeping inch by inch toward the rear of the *bashas.* A terrible weakness paralyzed Jerry. He wanted to go with them, but could not; he seemed to be pinned to the ground by tiny stakes, like Gulliver.

Chet Khin touched his arm, touched Jerry's gun, and made gestures signifying, "Stay here! Fire at the soldiers when we do!"

He nodded woodenly. The Kachin slipped away. Jerry was alone in the darkness. He could no longer see the Rangers—only the enemy. He laid his gun before him, in line with the campfire, and touched the trigger. He picked the man he was going to fire at first. But all at once he knew that he could not fire at him.

He was not ready to kill anyone! It seemed a violation of everything good to send a stutter of thirty-caliber bullets into those wine-warmed bodies at the campfire. But that was what he had been sent here to do. That was what the whole thing was about.

He saw a shadow flick across the ground behind a hut. Another shadow passed, like a bat zipping after an insect. The men were entering the *bashas* from the rear. Jerry raised the gun. It felt as clumsy as a broomstick; its outlines were completely unfamiliar. His fingers groped over the cold metal, found the trigger-guard, and felt for the trigger.

Suddenly a terrible clamor deafened him. His heart seemed to squeeze and then explode. The gun of its own volition had given a jerk in his hands. A jet of flame darted from the muzzle toward the campfire. A soldier screamed and put his hands over his face. The song died in a chorus of shouts and screams.

Jerry tore his hand from the gun and stared at it. He could not believe he had squeezed the trigger.

Around the fire several men sprang up, seizing rifles from the ground. Two other men fell forward. Then, unexpectedly, there was a white-hot flash of fire in the core of the campfire itself as it erupted like a volcano. Embers were hurled everywhere. Jerry heard the peculiar gurgling drumfire of a burp gun and saw its flashes from the door of a *basha.* Other weapons opened up and the sharp flash-and-roar of grenades followed one another.

But the Japanese had scattered among the huts, their own weapons opening up on the *bashas.* Jerry saw one of them throw a grenade into a hut, and there was a flash of fire an instant later. The latticed sides of the hut were blown open. He could not tell whether there had been any Kachins in the hut; but if there had been, they would be dead now, and he would be to blame.

He stood up, shaken. Somehow he found himself moving toward the *bashas,* firing his gun. Somewhere in the village a gun opened up with a peculiar, soft *pup-pup-pup* of firing—shots that were accompanied by little silken slashes of air as a string of bullets passed him.

Then he heard cries nearby, and saw a small figure in a big Aussie hat gesturing to him. It was Chet Khin, pausing in his own flight to make sure Jerry was fleeing too. Jerry muttered, "Okay! Okay!" and started to turn. Something landed on the ground not far from his feet. He stared, fascinated, at a tiny fizzing ember of light. Then he fell back with a shout.

The grenade exploded.

Jerry was already falling. He was stunned by the impact of the explosion on his eardrums. Even his stomach felt the jarring report. There was a warm, watery sensation in his side, and when he put his hand over it, it came away wet.

He clambered up and began to run. I can't be hurt badly, he told himself, or I couldn't run. It's just a flesh wound. *Just a flesh wound, ma'am,* he thought, with lightheaded whimsy. *I've been shot up worse and took in a hoedown.* But he ran, as if proving to himself that he was all right.

Someone had him by the arm—Chicken again, guiding him back to the rendezvous. A few dozen yards more and they were there.

Back in the brush, Captain Cork counted his men hastily. "We're short two boys," he said grimly, then spoke some words of Jingpaw to Chet Khin. "A grenade got them," he said. "How'd you make out, fella?" he asked Jerry.

"I was scared silly," Jerry panted. His lungs were scorched inside; his mouth was watering profusely. "I guess I tipped our hand. I fired my gun accidentally."

"I thought it sounded like a carbine. Say, you're bleeding!"

"Shrapnel," Jerry said. "Just in the hip, I think."

Cork peered at him. "Boy, if I lose you, they'll never lend me another translator! Let's get out of here."

They traveled by trails Jerry could not even see. Thorny bamboo slashed at his hands. He floundered along behind the captain until they emerged on the main trail. It seemed wide enough for an automobile. Here, two miles from the village, they stopped for a break.

Captain Cork put out security guards and came to look at Jerry's wound by flashlight. The wound was in his hip, just below his belt, deep in the muscle. Cork dusted sulfa powder into it and applied a compress bandage.

"What about the song?" he asked, as he worked.

"The song? Oh!" Jerry had forgotten how the thing had started. He made an effort to remember. "Some of the words were, 'Though my body decay in Guadalcanal, my spirit will persist in defense of the homeland.' I don't see how that helps much," he added apologetically.

Pat Cork beamed. "You don't, eh? It helps to this extent—it tells us they've had reinforcements! You see, the heroes of Singapore—Tanaka's Eighteenth Division, the bunch we've been fighting up to now—never set foot on Guadalcanal! They took Singapore, Malaya, and Burma—but they never got out of Asia. It's bad news, of course, but at least we know about it. Now, then, we'll see what can be done about getting you out of here in the morning."

As the numbness of initial shock wore off, Jerry's wound began to make itself felt. One of the Kachins made him a crutch of bamboo, and he limped along the trail, sweating profusely and almost sobbing with the ragged pain tearing at his nerves. After a couple of hours, it seemed, they heard one of those brash, peremptory birdcalls which came so suddenly and surprisingly from the jungle. But this was after-hours for the particular bird whose call had come to them, and they knew it was a sentry: they had reached the group they had left behind earlier. In a few minutes they were at the bivouac. Cork insisted on Jerry's lying down at once, and he changed the blood-soaked bandage. While he worked, he talked.

"There's a teak forest a little way from here where a boy can shinny up a tree in the morning with the aerial. The pilot will probably be ranging around looking for us anyway."

"But where can he land?" Jerry asked uneasily.

Cork chuckled. "He claims he can land an L-plane in a bird's nest—and he may have to this time. But we'll find a spot for him."

His confidence was warming. Relaxing on the poncho which had been spread for him, Jerry felt, for the first time, that he might actually get out of the jungle alive. And there came back to him, for some reason, the remembrance of taking forbidden pictures at Savage, and charting the ship's position. They were like childhood memories. It was hard to believe he had ever been young enough to find them important.

The pain-killing shot Cork administered brought a delicious lassitude, in which memories swirled like smoke in his mind—family parties at Christmas and New Year's—picnics at the beach when he was very small. . . . And thinking these things, he slipped exhausted into sleep.

CHAPTER 16

# "Mission Completed"

Early the following day an L-plane was heard zooming around. Captain Cork hurried to attempt radio contact. The radio was a walkie-talkie to which had been connected a hand-cranked magneto, a lightweight outfit of short range, but independent of batteries. They had moved to the edge of the teak forest where the Kachins had run an aerial up through the big leafless trees.

It was dusty in the forest, this being the dry season, and Jerry lay on a mattress of big, dead leaves. He was scarcely aware of the pain in his wounded hip; the captain had given him another pain-killing shot with a first-aid syrette.

Soon Cork came over and announced cheerfully, "I've made contact! Now we've got to shove off. The boys say there's hard sand along a dry river a couple of miles from here where he can land. They're trying to spot it for him now. He should be there by the time we make it ourselves."

Jerry noticed suddenly that Cork was shaking—trembling with an ague that made his teeth rattle. "What's the matter?" he asked, concerned. "I think you're sicker than I am!"

Cork smiled. "Forgot to take my atabrine," he said. "Now I'll have the malaria shakes for a while. Atabrine won't keep you from getting malaria—nothing in God's green jungle will—but it suppresses the symptoms, at least, so you can keep going. You get used to it."

While they moved on through the jungle toward the river, he described to Jerry some of the nuisances, as he called them, besetting the jungle fighter: "dinky" fever—dengue, or breakbone; five types of malaria, two of which are fatal; typhus fever, caused by mites which bore into the skin; ghastly Naga sores, caused by another insect; and of course dysentery.

"But we keep going," he finished good-naturedly.

Jerry limped along on his jungle crutch until they reached the river. From the tangled growth of its banks they searched up and down the river bed for some time before moving into the open. A wide, level shelf of sand ran out to a thin stream of clear water, and on this sand a red T of rayon parachute cloth had been spread to attract the pilot's attention. After a time they heard his engine humming in the distance. The sound strengthened, and suddenly broke with a roar as the L-plane came in view, flying upstream just above the treetops. The pilot waggled his wings and veered away to come in at the strip at lower speed. Jerry felt a relief that was as soothing as warm water.

"In a couple of weeks," Captain Cork predicted, "you'll be able to rejoin your outfit. Bet you'll be hiking the Ledo Road with your own bunch."

Shamefully, Jerry realized he lacked the enthusiasm of going into combat with his own bunch that he had had before. At the same time, however, he felt a great desire to be with Russ and Ben and Matsumoto again, to try to impart to them what it was like to be in combat, to give them time to steel themselves for that shocking noise of weapons and the screams of wounded men. Or could it be done, actually? Could anyone make another person understand what war was who hadn't experienced it?

The plane swerved in, dropped fast, lost speed, and touched down. It lurched along the sand and came to a stop. Heaven help us if he can't get out again! thought Jerry, watching the wheels settle into the sand. The Air Force man came from the plane, stretching as he walked. He looked at Jerry's crutch with sour amusement.

"Look at you! Some guys just can't keep out of trouble! I leave you alone for one night—and you get shot up!"

"Come on—off you go," Captain Cork said quickly. "There may be other patrols in the area besides the one we tangled with last night."

He helped Jerry to the plane. The pain was coming back now, long, deep stabs of agony. He was sweating, his hands clutching wads of his clothing as he strained against it. The sergeant climbed into the plane and fastened his seat belt.

"Wait a minute," Cork said. "It won't prove anything for you to fight that pain all the way back to Margherita." He took a syrette from his first-aid kit, fumbling it out with his feverish fingers, pushed up Jerry's sleeve, and gave him another shot. "That'll hold you. Good luck"—he smiled—"and thanks."

"I'm sorry about last night," Jerry said impulsively. "If I hadn't started firing—"

"Somebody else would have," Pat Cork chuckled.

With the aid of the Kachins, the liaison plane was turned about. Looking down at the slight figures dressed in green, Jerry was reminded of junior Robin Hoods. "Cross your fingers," the pilot said tightly. He gunned the engine; the Kachins began pushing at the wing-struts to help the plane get started. Lurching down the sand, it bounced into the air, settled back with a jolt, bounced higher, and was suddenly air-borne, like a kite caught by a breeze. The pilot swerved it into midstream where there were no trees to reach for its wings; he thrust the throttle all the way forward and eased the stick back. Bouncing on the air drafts, the plane roared along just above the clear, cold water. Suddenly it lifted on an updraft and was swung high above the forest. It climbed fast, light and frail as paper, and the pilot sank back in the seat with a sigh.

"Every time I do that," he said, "I get fifty more white hairs. I'll be gray as granite before the rains come."

Jerry saw that his face was slick with perspiration. He realized he had not been worried, himself. But this was not courage, he knew. It was partly ignorance and partly the mental fog of pain and drugs. He settled back, looked out over the endless Burmese jungle, and let drowsiness enfold him like a dream.

# CHAPTER 17

# The Four Winds Code

Jerry was in the tent hospital at Margherita, near the head of the Ledo Road, for three weeks. He turned in the documents he had taken from the flier, but kept the book of poetry. While he was bedridden, he read it sometimes. His wound healed quickly. It was a time of rest and contemplation, a healing of his mind as well as his body. But soon he began to grow restless.

One day he said to a medical officer, "I think I'm about ready to move out, doctor. My hip feels pretty good."

"You've got at least a month of convalescing ahead. But don't worry—you won't do your convalescing here. You're already slated to ship out."

The following day a special order came through listing Jerry with some other men about to be flown back from the staging center. The hospital at Margherita was an evacuation hospital, where wounded or sick men were treated just long enough to enable them to be moved to a rear-area hospital. They were loaded into a C-47 ambulance plane which took off to the west.

In a few hours they landed outside a big city on a broad plain. The copilot came back from the cabin. "New

Delhi," he said. "Don't forget to salute the generals. This is the Big Town in the CBI!"

Jerry spent a few days in the big Allied hospital before he was released as an out-patient with orders to check in for examination every day. While he was there, he learned things about New Delhi. This big, old city of northern India was not only the capital of the country, but was the headquarters of the United States Army and Air Force in the China-Burma-India theater of war. General Stilwell's headquarters were here, though "Vinegar Joe" spent little time in the city. He preferred his jungle headquarters on the Ledo Road. There was a big prisoner-of-war compound in Old Delhi, the walled city which was part of Delhi itself, and there was a building like an old mud-walled castle where the "Language Pool" of Allied Translation and Intelligence Service was quartered. On his first day out of the hospital, Jerry reported here.

He strolled down the long, arched walk forming the front of the building. After so long in the field, it was queer to see so many officers in crisp suntan uniforms—everything up to and including generals—and even to see Red Cross girls and a few nurses. He could not walk ten yards without saluting an officer or smiling at a girl. At last he saw a sign:

ALLIED TRANSLATION &
INTELLIGENCE SERVICE

He entered a big high-ceilinged room. Far above his head a fan stirred the warm air. There were wide, unscreened windows and solid-looking doors opening off the central office. To his pleasure, Jerry saw that every desk in the room was occupied by a Nisei.

He handed his orders to Sergeant Nomura, who smiled and said, "You took the scenic route getting here, Harada. We've heard about you."

"How?" Jerry asked in surprise.

"You can't keep secrets among Niseis."

Nomura led Jerry back through the room. At every desk a Nisei was working on a document of some kind. Some were reading captured Japanese diaries, flown in from all over the CBI. The Japanese were inveterate keepers of diaries, and much was learned from their private remarks about their officers, their morale, and their yearnings to be home. Other Niseis were translating letters or typing up copies of them in English, while still other men were translating captured field orders and technical manuals, or examining maps.

Sergeant Nomura stopped before a big, littered desk on which was a plaque reading:

LIEUTENANT ANDOW
CHIEF OF SECTION

A solid-looking Japanese with short, muscular arms looked Jerry over closely. Lieutenant Andow was sober in manner, with a direct gaze. He had a round head with a black butch haircut and a corrugated brow.

"Have a seat," he told Jerry.

Sergeant Nomura went back to his desk and Jerry pulled a chair up to Andow's desk.

"You didn't waste any time getting in action," the lieutenant said. "I've been hanging around here a year, and I haven't been out of Delhi."

"Well—combat's not all it's cracked up to be," Jerry said.

"I'd like to try it, anyway. The Pool, here, is kind of like a hotel. They check in and they check out—anywhere in the CBI. As soon as I get a man trained, they steal him from me."

He opened a folder and glanced into it. "According to your file, you're a handy man to have around. I wish I were going to have you longer."

This was Jerry's first indication that he would not be in Delhi forever. "Am I slated to ship out?"

"You're still being carried as assigned to the 5307th, but on temporary duty with ATIS."

Jerry became thoughtful. He reflected on the quiet days in the hospital, the pleasant, airy room he shared here with five other men; and then he thought of the jungle with its leeches and mites and malaria and sudden death around every turn. How anxious was he, actually, to go back? The unworthy thought shamed him.

"Do you like code work?" Andow asked.

"I haven't had any practical experience—just the training."

"I think I'll try you out, anyway. We're always looking for a flash code man." He grinned.

Andow escorted him to another office, where a Nisei

named Clarence Yamagata was working. "Clarence, I've brought you a boy to go out for coffee while you pretend to work," Andow said with a smile. "This is Jerry Harada."

Jerry shook hands with Yamagata. Andow moved to the door. "Clarence will give you something to work on. By the way, did you know you're up for a couple of medals?"

Jerry was stunned. "Medals?"

Andow smiled. "The Purple Heart, of course, for forgetting to duck. Plus a Bronze Star for meritorious action; and you've gone up in rating to corporal."

"You're kidding!" Jerry said. He was staggered. "Why, I was scared stiff. All I did was question a captured flier, and then go along on a patrol. In fact, I fired my carbine too soon and nearly spoiled the show!"

"Don't ask me," Andow said. "Personally, I think it will make good reading in the papers back on the West Coast—'Nisei gets medal for heroism!' Of course I agree that it's probably bunk"—he winked at Clarence Yamagata —"but it won't hurt to give a few Caucasians the idea that all Niseis are heroes."

Still Jerry felt a flush of shame, almost of anger, as he recalled his fears that night. "But why did they pick me? Those little Kachins who were leading me around are entitled to medals for breakfast—not to mention their C.O."

"Ours not to reason why—" the lieutenant suggested. But Jerry sensed that he was somehow pleased at Jerry's honest displeasure at being cited.

Jerry did not have to pretend modesty, for he was

thinking, What if I freeze up again the next time I get in combat?—and the papers print *that* story! "Nisei 'Hero' Responsible for Loss of Patrol!" Uneasy lay the head that wore a garland, he decided.

Yamagata introduced Jerry to the work.

"We've got a lot of things going," he explained, "but the biggest thing right now is the Four Winds Code. When we break that, we'll start sinking Jap ships by the dozen, and bombing airfields before their fighters can even take off. We've got stems and pieces of it, but not enough. I've worked on it so long myself I'm going stale. I think I'll put you on it while I go back to a numbers code I've got almost a complete book on. Of course, as fast as we get a lead on something, we send it back to Washington."

There were encoding and decoding machines to help with the work, but most of it was plain, old-fashioned puzzle-solving. Jerry worked at it for a week. Decoding would have been hard enough in English, but in Japanese it was incalculably more difficult. To begin with, a certain symbol might be read one way by one person and completely differently by another. The symbol for *kamikaze* could also be read *shimpu*. Because of this, a cryptographer might blunder along on a dozen false leads before finding the right one—if he ever found it.

Jerry made no progress at all. He felt humiliated and blocked. More than ever he regretted the citation for a medal; it made him look like a hometown hero who broke down ludicrously in the big leagues. He threw out all his work and started over. In a short time he was at dead end again.

"How are you making out?" Yamagata asked him one morning, a week later.

"I'm losing ground," Jerry admitted.

"Maybe you need a break. Do you want to talk to the lieutenant about doing something else for a while?"

"Can you spare me?" Jerry asked ironically.

He told Lieutenant Andow, "It looks as if I'm not your flash code man, Lieutenant. What do you think about my going back to my outfit now?"

"What do you want to do—get all the medals in the Army?" Andow joked. "You'll go back when the medics certify you as fit, which you aren't now. I'll tell you what—we've got a lot of prisoners over in Old Delhi. Want to have a try at interrogation?"

"Sure do!" Jerry was excited by the idea.

"All right. Take this pass over to the prison. They'll assign you somebody to work on. It's a waste of time, usually, because all the prisoners have been interrogated three or four times before we ever get them. But we keep trying. We've got a nice, choice admiral we don't know what to do with, and any number of colonels. Also some actresses!"

"You're kidding!"

"No, sir. Real live actresses and geishas. Part of a troupe who'd travel around putting on entertainments for the officers. They were on a ship bound for Manila when it was sunk by one of our warships. Why don't you question one of them?"

Jerry frowned. "What would an actress know about war plans?"

"Maybe nothing. But some officer might have told her something. Or she might be able to point out a V.I.P. in the prison."

Interested, Jerry said, "All right. I can't do any worse than I did at breaking down codes."

CHAPTER 18

# F'saya

Jerry took the prison pass over to the old city and was admitted into the prison compound. Hundreds of dispirited men in baggy uniforms circulated in a central yard. The guards told Jerry that most of them were good prisoners, eager to please. He went through an arched gate into another section of the prison and explained to the prison matron Lieutenant Andow's suggestion that he talk to one of the geishas. The matron, a British woman, asked Jerry to wait in a small visiting room off her office. Presently she returned with a small, very pretty girl wearing a dark-blue prison dress. The girl made the customary polite curtsy. Jerry did not know whether to bow from the waist as in a school play, or shake hands with her.

"*O-hayo*," he said. "Good morning."

"This is Fusaye Nishamura," the matron declared, pronouncing the name correctly—*F'saya.* "She is one of the most cooperative girls in the compound, so you might start with her. We have eighteen now."

The girl had an oval face with very narrow eyes and soft, fawn-colored skin. Her black hair had been cut in the

Western style when she was imprisoned. She wore it in a long, glossy bob. She was slender, dainty, and graceful.

"Sit down, F'saya," the matron said. The girl glanced at her, disturbed, and murmured a protest. "All right!—You sit down first," the matron told Jerry. "This girl had her training in the Old Country. She wouldn't *think* of sitting down while you're still standing up. Now, don't let her charm you into helping her to escape!"

Jerry sat at one side of a small, white-painted table. The girl took the chair opposite him, moving mincingly, and waited demurely with her hands folded in her lap. The matron went out and closed the door.

The two young Japanese sat in silence. After a while Jerry cleared his throat rather pompously. He had no idea how to begin. Feeling it was a businesslike thing to do, he laid his notebook on the table and placed his pencil beside it. Then he realized it was probably not a good thing to do at all: prisoners tended to freeze up when they saw all their statements being written down.

"Your name is F'saya Nishamura?" he said.

"Yes—sir." The girl's eyes glanced up briefly, then dropped to her lap. They were not so narrowed now. She seemed to know how to use her eyes to hide behind or to charm with.

"How old are you, F'saya?"

"Nineteen, sir."

"You don't have to call me 'sir.' You embarrass me. I'm not used to girls being so polite."

Gazing at him with quick interest, the girl asked, "Girls are not polite in America?"

"Oh, yes. Only in a different way. For instance, a man never sits down before a woman does. The woman is always seated first."

"How barbarous!" F'saya exclaimed.

"It's the custom."

"Do they wear their hair like mine?" the girl asked, passing her hand over her hair.

"Pretty much. My sister wears hers almost the same way. They call it 'page boy.' "

"But it is like a man's, then!" the girl protested.

Jerry smiled. "Oh, no—not to a man, it isn't. But I guess you were sorry to lose your beautiful hair, weren't you?"

"I thought of killing myself. I felt shamed. Yet now I find this style very comfortable in the heat. It is so hot here in India."

"Do you have a fan?"

"No, sir—Lieutenant . . . what do I call you?" she asked, very disarming in her helplessness.

"Michio, if you want." He thought it might establish a more comfortable relationship if she used his Japanese name. "I'll see that you get a fan, then. Would you like cigarettes?"

"No, Michio, I thank you."

"Where did you live, in Japan?"

"In Osaka."

"Osaka!" Jerry exclaimed. "I have an aunt and uncle in Osaka. I lived there for a year when I was fourteen."

"Ah, so!" F'saya's eyes opened wide, becoming glossy black ovals in her tawny face. "You did not like Osaka?"

"I liked it fine. But my home has always been California."

"Then you know Hollywood?" F'saya touched her throat.

"Sure—I only lived ten miles from Hollywood. I've been through the studios and seen a lot of the stars."

F'saya's dream was to become a moving picture actress. She told him so with animation. Then she added, dispiritedly, "But all that is over, now. There will never be a moving picture industry again."

"Why not—don't you think Japan will win the war and have everything she ever had?" Jerry asked.

"No. I do not think so, sir—Michio."

"Why not?"

"Because—well, because . . ."

Jerry leaned closer. He peered carefully into the neat little Oriental face, wondering whether she was trapping him, or he was trapping her. "Because she has been losing ground for a year?" he prompted.

"Because of that, and—and other things."

"Then it would be best if Japan lost the war quickly, wouldn't it?" Jerry asked.

The girl looked away, at the door, at the table, at Jerry, and then at her lap. "I don't know . . . I don't know. . . ."

"I suppose it's foolish to ask a girl if she knows any military secrets," Jerry suggested.

"Ah, so?" F'saya challenged. "Be sure that if a geisha knew a secret, she would keep it."

"Even if it cost Japan thousands of lives?"

"I do not think this is true," the girl protested. "So many millions of prayers are rising in the smoke of incense that I think they must be heard."

Jerry shrugged. "Buddha didn't hear the prayer of a young flier I interrogated last month. He was a fine, intelligent man who wrote beautiful poetry. But he died in the jungle. Do you know why he died, F'saya? Because his plane was made of wood and fabric—like a kite. He crashed, for no reason except that Japan has run out of war materials."

The girl's face grew wary as she studied him. "I do not believe this. I do not think there was any such flier."

Jerry pulled a small book from his pocket and opened it to the flyleaf. He read aloud the inscription: "*To our son, Hiroshi—from his parents.*" He handed the book to the girl. "This was his. Would you like it?"

F'saya read the inscription for herself, opened the book and glanced at a poem, then closed it and laid it in her lap. She smiled gratefully at him. "Thank you. I hope the matron will let me keep it."

"She will—if I tell her to. Will you do something for me, now?"

The lustrous oval eyes gazed at him. "What do you wish me to do?"

"I want you to tell me something. Are there any prisoners here who were important men in Japan? Anyone who could give us information which might help end the war sooner?"

The girl inspected the book again, and Jerry thought she was not going to answer. Then she murmured, "Ask for Udo-san."

"Who is he?"

"He was foreman of a big aircraft plant in Japan."

"In what city?"

"I do not know. But it was a big plant, and very secret. It was in the country. One-third of Japan's production of fighter planes was there, Udo-san told me."

"How do you know about him?"

Jerry began to throb with excitement, knowing how close he was to something really big, for some day soon the Allies would have airfields close enough to Japan to start regular bombing raids. Information regarding future targets would then be of great importance.

"I helped nurse him," F'saya was saying. "He was captured in Nanking by the Chinese. They tortured him and starved him. He told me only a little about himself—but he told the Chinese nothing. Probably he will tell you nothing."

"He might tell you, though, F'saya—"

"How could he? We never talk together."

"I could arrange for you to talk together."

F'saya shook her head. "Japanese men do not talk serious things with Japanese girls."

"At least he might tell you where the plant is."

Again she shook her head. "I will not be a spy."

Jerry was growing desperate. "Then tell him what I've told you—about the kind of planes Japanese boys are flying today! Tell him what Hiroshi Sato told me—that hundreds of young fliers go out to attack warships, and never come back. If you tell him these things, he might talk to you."

F'saya bowed her head. "Very well. I try."

After the girl was taken back to the women's courtyard, Jerry talked to the matron.

"How can we arrange for her to talk to one of the male prisoners? His name is Udo—he was a V.I.P. before he went into the army, and she's agreed to try to get information from him."

"Simple," the Englishwoman said. "We'll put him back in the prison hospital. He's still suffering tuberculosis after his stay with the Chinese. The girl can help nurse him."

Several times during the next two weeks Jerry talked to F'saya. She was not sure whether she was making progress or not. But one day she said, "Please bring a drawing board and paper. He asks for them."

Jerry did so, and three days later she brought them to the little query-room. A beautifully detailed map of a Japanese town and countryside filled one sheet of paper. A railroad and seaport were plainly marked. The other sheet was a complete layout of an aircraft plant. Jerry hurried with them to Lieutenant Andow. Andow studied them.

"Very pretty," he said. "But how do we know he isn't just trying to get us to drop bombs on a fishing village?"

They discovered a note pinned to the back of the plans, but it had little effect on Andow's doubts.

HONORED SIRS:

KNOWING THAT MY REVERED FATHERLAND MUST EVENTUALLY BE DEFEATED IN THIS STRUGGLE, I HAND YOU THESE MAPS, IN THE HOPE OF ENDING THE WAR SOONER.

UDO.

The following day, however, they had convincing assurance that the note and the plans were legitimate. The prisoner was found dead in his cot. He had cut a large vein in his leg and had bled to death during the night.

Jerry was shocked. Yet he knew that to the Japanese there was nothing dishonorable about taking one's life. When life, for one reason or another, became a burden, it was considered perfectly proper to end it.

Jerry was kept on interrogation duty. Somewhat to his surprise, he found most of the prisoners cooperative. They told what they knew, but they knew very little. In the Japanese army soldiers were led to battle like oxen, where they were expected to fight like tigers. In view of their low station, it was surprising that they could be whipped up to the screaming banzai attacks for which they were famous.

For two pleasant weeks, he was host to a captured Japanese admiral, taking him about New Delhi, trying to impress him with the kindness of the Allies toward their prisoners, and letting him see enough of the tremendous volume of war material passing through Delhi to convince him that America's ability to supply her troops, and those of her allies, was inexhaustible. It was useless. The little middle-aged man responded politely to all innocuous questions, but said, "I do not know," whenever a pointed query was directed at him.

Jerry had some bad experiences, too.

One of them was with Yasuda, a tense and bitter man who had been in the Japanese intelligence branch. Yasuda had driven a bayonet into his abdomen when he was captured—but he recovered. Refusing to give even his serial number, he was sent to Delhi for further interrogation. On the plane, he swallowed a spoon and nearly choked to death. Jerry interviewed him in his mud-walled cell a couple of days after he arrived.

Yasuda stood against the wall, glaring at Jerry, who sat on his cot wondering how to get through the cold steel of hatred. Outside, a guard waited.

"You were in intelligence, Yasuda-san," Jerry said. "How many men were in your unit?"

Yasuda crossed his arms and stared at him. He was a tall man, nearly six feet in height, with a shaved head, a few moles, long ears, and a very hard chin.

"We have heard that General Tanaka is in disfavor because he has failed to take the city of Imphal," Jerry continued. "Is it true?"

"I would bite my tongue out before I told you anything," Yasuda said slowly.

"You are very patriotic—but blind. Japan is losing the war. She has not won a major battle for months."

"Tides turn," snapped Yasuda.

"We hear stories of a '*kamikaze* corps'—a group of young fliers dedicated to suicidal attacks on Allied ships. This does not sound like the strategy of a powerful foe."

"The divine wind," said Yasuda, "will blow you off the sea." The *divine wind* was the Japanese name for the Special Naval Attack Force—the *kamikaze* group. The term referred to a hurricane which had once saved Japan from invasion by destroying all of an invader's warships. And now this same sort of tactics—a hurricane of explosive-carrying planes designed to destroy ships by crashing into them—was expected to sweep the Allies from the sea by a latter-day *kamikaze*, or "divine wind." Evidence was increasing that such a force was being trained.

Jerry smiled. Yasuda did not seem to be aware of having just given something away. "Then," he said, "there is such a force?" He was pleased at having found substantiation, at last, for the rumor.

Yasuda's jaws clenched hard. Jerry looked down at his notebook, considering how to proceed. Then he heard a curious, strangling sound from where Yasuda stood. The prisoner sank to his knees. Jerry went toward him quickly.

"Guard!" he called.

As he approached him, Yasuda opened his mouth—to reveal, horribly, a tongue nearly severed. He had made good his promise to bite his tongue out before he told Jerry anything. Sickness flooded Jerry and he turned Yasuda over to the guards and summoned a doctor.

. . . To his immense surprise, a letter written in beautiful Japanese brush-characters came to him from Yasuda a week later. The intelligence man was again recovering.

*Buddha does not wish me to die,* he wrote. *Therefore it must be that he wishes me to aid the Americans for the eventual good of Nippon. I was attached to General Tanaka's Eighteenth Division. Tanaka is in disfavor but has not been removed. There are new forces in Burma. Attacks will soon be made on Imphal and Kohima. To win Burma, destroy Rangoon.*

A few days after this, the clerk from the message center placed an order on Jerry's desk.

"T/5 Michio Harada is relieved of temporary assignment and duty with his unit ATIS and will return to duty with 2nd Battalion, 5307th Composite Unit (Provisional), Margherita, India."

A wave of goose-flesh ran up his forearms. He could smell the bitter-sweetness of the jungle again; could feel the weight of pack-straps galling his shoulders. He put his hand on his side and felt the still-tender spot where the shrapnel had torn into his body. He remembered—with uneasiness and shame—the night at the village, when he had nearly spoiled the attack. He wondered whether in those terrible minutes, he had learned anything besides his limitations.

But whatever was ahead for him, he was pleased and excited at the prospect of rejoining his old outfit.

## CHAPTER 19

# The Road

At Margherita, he left the plane. "You can catch a ride with one of the trucks going down The Road," the pilot told him.

He wandered from the field in search of the motor pool, feeling lost. Trucks slammed through their gears, careening up and down the road. He saw engineer and signal outfits drilling with their special equipment, and a few combat units in the field. An ambulance with a red cross on its top lumbered in and headed for the hospital—the only area Jerry knew.

He asked several men where the Second Battalion was, and all gave him the same answer: Second had gone "down The Road." Everyone referred to "The Road." The construction of the Ledo Road was easily the most important project of its kind at the time in Burma. Important or not, it was up to him to find his own outfit on The Road. There had been a couple of battles down The Road already—at villages bearing the exotic names of Nzang Ga and Lanem Ga. Details were few. The actions hadn't amounted to much, it was said. Only a few dead.

At Ledo, Jerry caught a ride with a Chinese truck driver leaving for Shing, as the troops around Margherita called the village of Shingbwiyang, near General Stilwell's jungle headquarters. They had not gone a hundred yards when he became convinced that he would never survive the ride. The Chinese soldier drove furiously, a cigarette fuming in his lips like a punk-stick, changing gears with a shrill scream of metal teeth, and frequently running so close to the edge of the cliff that clods of red earth were thrown over. It was no comfort to see the rusting hulks of trucks which had gone over.

There were many Chinese troops marching down The Road. Jerry learned that they were following the Americans, occupying in strength the points won by the Marauders in their swift surprise raid on the Japanese-held Kamaing Road. The Kamaing Road branched south off the Ledo Road at Shing. Thus, won by the Marauders and held by the Chinese, the Kamaing Road would furnish the means of swift transportation of troops and supplies for both groups as they penetrated deeper into Burma. Southeast of Shing, the Chinese Expeditionary Force under Stilwell had been fighting for several months.

The Chinese troops always seemed to be in good spirits. They waved at the trucks and grinned. From what Jerry had heard, this was one of their failings as soldiers: they lacked the grim aggressiveness needed by combat troops. They were enjoying their American supplies, though they persisted in an all-rice diet. Their cooks trotted along with a big cooking pot at one end of a pole across their shoulders, and a gunny sack of supplies at the other end, dressed in shorts and undershirts and resembling distance runners.

It was 112 miles to Shingbwiyang, and Jerry rode in six trucks in three days before he made it. The Road was a mighty, crimson slash through the mountains, hairpinning down one side of a canyon, switchbacking up the other side, topping chilly divides where cold mist fell, then dropping precipitously to jungle where the heat was moist and suffocating. Along the way were machine shops where broken-down trucks and graders waited to be repaired. Hospitals took care of road casualties, and at intervals an encampment of Negro engineers would be seen.

Along The Road, too, were grim mementos of the refugees who had fled from Burma before the Japanese two years ago. Beside the streams were whitened skeletons of the thousands of men, women, and children who had fallen to starvation, exhaustion, and disease.

Jerry traveled in a semicomatose condition, shaken so that his back was sore from contact with the seat. Dust lay in drifts on his uniform. As he climbed into a truck for the final few miles into Shing, he heard what sounded like thunder. He asked the Negro driver whether it was thunder or artillery.

"That's firing, Corporal," the driver assured him. "Not our troops, though—the Chinese are trying to push the Japs down the Kamaing Road. Where you heading?"

"I'm trying to find my outfit—the Second Battalion."

"They went through about a week ago. I'll leave you off at headquarters company tonight. They'll tell you how to find 'em."

Late that afternoon the truck emerged from the mountains onto the broad Hukawng Valley. Jerry smiled at the beauty of it. Across the valley wound the gleaming system of rivers which formed the headwaters of the Chindwin. In the red light of sunset, a low mountain chain could be discerned at the southern end of the valley.

"See that ridge, yonder?" the driver asked. "That's Jambu Bum—what a name! Jambu Bum Ridge. Way I get it, the Marauders are making for the ridge. They'll try to cross it and keep pushing down the Kamaing Road."

The driver dropped Jerry at headquarters company area and he hunted up the orderly room. A clerk stopped typing a laundry list when he presented himself. There was a feeling of clutter and movement about the whole camp. Crowded into the wood-floored tent were a dozen tables where clerks were typing up lists and letters.

"I'm trying to catch up with Second Battalion," Jerry told the clerk.

The clerk sketched a little map on a piece of paper, then drew an X on it. "That's us." He drew a straight line to bisect a curving line on the map. "That's where the regiment crossed the Tawang River yesterday." Bringing the line on to another river, he said, "They should bivouac near this one, the Tanai, tonight. But there hasn't been any radio contact today and we don't know where they are. What's your unit?"

"I & R platoon."

"Oh-oh," the clerk said.

"What's the matter?" Jerry asked, uneasily.

"Going to be hard to find. I & R goes out ahead, you know, like the bumpers on a car. But we'll get you there. . . ."

"Is the country clear in between?"

"Not so clear that we're sending men out alone to find their outfits. There's a pioneer and demolition platoon going out in the morning. You'll travel with them. Hungry?" he asked.

"I could eat."

"Head over to the hospital detachment mess—best food in *this* camp."

As he ate, Jerry could hear the far-off shaking rumble of artillery, and wondered if it meant the Marauders were engaged with the Japanese. But since the Chinese were fighting the Japanese nearby it might be part of that action.

After dinner he was sent to a *basha* where the pioneer and demolition platoon was quartered. He spread his blanket on the bamboo floor and settled down to try to sleep. Men kept coming in, yawning, to grope about for their blankets. Jerry talked to a man lying next to him.

"How did they happen to leave you behind?" he asked.

"I guess we were an afterthought," the soldier murmured. "There must be more demolitions work than they were looking for—pillboxes and bunkers."

"I hear there've been a couple of actions already."

"Just patrol clashes. There was a little battle at Nzang Ga. The Japs tried a trailblock that didn't work. The Marauders killed a half dozen of them. Then there was an ambush at Lanem Ga. They killed one Marauder there."

"What battalion?" Jerry asked.

"Second. I & R platoon."

Jerry was chilled and sobered. One of the men he had trained with, had come across the Pacific with, had gotten it. It might have been the veteran he had talked with that day when the plane flew in for an interpreter. He might have slept in this same *basha* on the way to his death. Solemnly, Jerry wondered whether it was all decided in advance, and they were just acting out a play written before they ever went into battle.

In the black pre-dawn, they crawled out of their blankets and made ready to march. The lieutenant in charge of the platoon gave the order to leave all nonessential equipment. "No blankets, no mess kits—we'll be carrying all our food, now, and you'll find it's heavy."

They had breakfast—their last hot meal—and struck east on a trail that branched off the Kamaing Road. A few miles down the road the Chinese were slowly pushing the Japanese southward through the jungle. That was the source of all the artillery firing. As they marched that day, Jerry began to picture the action that was shaping up.

It was not so different from football. The Chinese and Japanese armies formed the opposing scrimmage lines. The Marauders were the Chinese backfield, and they were trying to run around left end. If they cut in too soon, of course, they would smash into the scrimmage line. So the I & R platoons would make little probing stabs at the jungle every so often to learn whether they had marched far enough east to have cleared left end—only it was called the enemy's flank, of course.

As soon as they found the jungle free of Japanese, the main body of the Marauders would turn south behind the Japanese and try to set up a strong block on the Kamaing Road. They would ambush any truck or troop movements on the road, and then try to hold the position until the Chinese moved in in large numbers to occupy it in force.

Whoever the Second Battalion man was who had been killed, he had died in one of the stabs at the enemy's flank—when the Marauders had not yet cleared it.

In mid-afternoon they halted at the Tarung River. The stream flowed down a wide, twisting aisle of gravel where white boulders bore the high-water marks of the rainy season. But now the water was low, and they could trace over sand the path the Marauders had made in crossing. They waded to an island and found evidence that they had camped here the first night. Everyone hoped they would bivouac. But the lieutenant spoiled their hope that they had finished their first day's march.

"If a platoon can't outmarch three battalions, there's something wrong. On your feet."

Jerry was softer than he had realized. His feet had begun to blister; his shoulders were sore from the pack-straps.

He was physically and nervously exhausted. Moving down the narrow trail, they had to watch constantly for signs of ambush. Each man had a designated direction in which to look. The lead scout watched the forest to the right of the trail ahead; the second scout watched the left. The third studied the treetops to the right for possible snipers, while the fourth peered into the branches on the left. Positions were constantly rotated, so that the nerve strain and danger of heading the column was shared.

Just before dusk the lead scout suddenly began raising and lowering his rifle frantically. The column halted; the lieutenant moved up. The men stepped from the trail into the brush. Jerry, near the head of the column, could hear the scout whispering: "There's something up ahead, Lieutenant! I could hear 'em moving around!"

"It might be Chinese. We'll have to be careful."

Jerry went forward. There was a brassy taste of fear on his tongue. "Lieutenant!" he whispered. "I'll go ahead and call to them in Japanese. If they answer, they're not Chinese."

Resting on one knee, the lieutenant muttered, "Good idea. Go ahead. Two of us will cover you."

They moved out together, Jerry a few yards ahead; then the lieutenant and scout took up positions to cover him as he went on alone. Jerry heard nothing; he beckoned them on. In this manner they moved up fifty yards. Jerry could feel his muscles drawing tight; he was taking shallow, nervous breaths. Now he reached a turn. Looking down, he saw footprints in the wet soil. They were so recent that water was still oozing into them. He turned quickly to motion the other men up. He showed the lieutenant the bootprints. The lieutenant studied them.

"They aren't GI—that's for sure! What kind of boots do the Chinese wear? Or the Japs, for that matter?" he added, nervously. It was obviously his first experience in a combat situation.

Jerry looked the trail over cautiously, and started ahead once more. Suddenly, a soldier stepped from the jungle onto the trail a hundred feet ahead. He was a small man in a baggy uniform—definitely Oriental, but not definitely Japanese—and his back was to them. Almost choking on his excitement, Jerry gave the others the rifle signal to take up firing positions. The column had come up close behind them. Then he called in Japanese, "Hey, soldier! Where's the command post?"

The soldier turned. Jerry still could not tell whether he was Japanese or Chinese. Then the man smiled and motioned him on. Jerry called to him again. The soldier shook his head. Back in the jungle a fever-bird made its sudden, raucous call.

Suddenly the scout screamed, "*There they are!*"

A machine gun shattered the stillness like glass. Jerry heard bullets plopping into the muddy trail behind him. The Japanese soldier dived for cover. Jerry hit the ground and fired at him. He saw him convulse and lie struggling with his legs still on the trail. Behind him, the scout was firing his Tommy gun. Then the lieutenant's carbine added its smashing reports to the uproar, and Jerry followed the smoky passage of tracers into a high crotch of a tree. He saw the Japanese sniper now, clutching an automatic weapon as he sprayed bullets down upon the trail. An instant later he dropped the weapon. It came crashing down through the foliage. The sniper hung in the tree-crotch by a safety belt.

"Spread out—both sides of the trail!" the lieutenant shouted.

Jerry crawled into the jungle growth at the right and began working his way forward. He heard the lieutenant behind him. From time to time there would be a nervous burst of firing; but there was no more of the distinctive, soft stutter of the Nambu machine gun.

The lieutenant shouted angrily, "Cut that firing! Don't fire unless you've got a target!"

With one squad going out on each flank and a third following the trail, the platoon advanced cautiously through the forest.

It was nearly dark when the lieutenant reassembled the men. "I think we got them. The Jap was just trying to bring us into range. We'll do another mile and bivouac."

CHAPTER 20

# Under Fire

Next day the column moved on with an awareness of marching deeper into trouble. The men felt blind and deaf, half-suffocated by the silent walls of green on both sides of them. In the distance they could hear artillery pounding steadily, and from time to time the heavier *crump* of bombs dropped by dive bombers. They marched all day in tense silence, bivouacking that night in a meadow of man-high *kunai* grass.

On the following day they passed a Kachin village and found the grave of an American soldier. *Robert W. Landis,* the name on the little cross read. His dog tags hung on it. This was the Second Battalion man of whose death Jerry had heard. He remembered the man, an Ohioan.

Just after leaving the village, they found the trail turning due south. Their second bivouac was made in a dense stand of thorny bamboo. Jerry stood guard until midnight, shivering with nervousness at every sound. Will I ever get used to it? he wondered. He remembered newspaper pictures of battle-seasoned veterans, hollow-cheeked, tough-jawed men who looked equal to anything. It must take a long time to get that way, he thought, for every man in this platoon was jumpy and scared.

For three more days the demolition platoon pressed along the wet green aisles of the jungle, frightened and jumpy, bunching together for comfort although their real safety lay in keeping sufficiently far apart that a machine-gunner could not get more than one or two men at a burst. They were running out of food. From a distance the sounds of battle were increasing every hour—the cannonading of artillery and the deep throb of bombs.

"Something big going on," the lieutenant muttered. "They must have stirred up a hornet's nest when they tried to block the road."

"Maybe those Japs don't want to give up the road!" a soldier suggested.

"I don't blame them. It's their only means of supplying their main line of resistance. The Marauders have gotten behind them, all right. If they can't retake the road, they'll have to pull south of it. . . ."

On the last day before they reached the regiment, they commenced hearing the flat explosions of mortar-bursts. Then the crackle of small-arms fire came into earshot, and gray and black towers of smoke could be seen above the forest whenever the jungle permitted them to see beyond the green-black tunnel along which they marched. Now and then a dive bomber roared above the treetops, and shortly after they would hear the blast of a bomb.

The lieutenant halted the column. Jerry suspected that

he knew little more about how to proceed than the men did. If they kept on, they might blunder into a Japanese strong point, for it was possible that the Marauders had been surrounded. The cold terror was growing in him that they were a lost platoon—unable to join the regiment, unable to retreat. The lieutenant did the sensible thing: he sent scouts ahead to find out what was happening. Then he deployed the men in protective positions.

In two hours the scouts were back—with a Marauder from First Battalion. The Marauder had come to guide them in.

"There's a real one going on!" he exclaimed. "In fact, there's two. Second and Third have set up separate roadblocks. Both of them are having a devil of a time hanging onto them. I think Second's almost cut off!"

"Where's First?" asked the lieutenant.

"We're acting as rear guard and regimental reserve."

Cut off! The words had a final, end-of-the-game ring in Jerry's head as they hurried on. Cut off from help . . . from supplies . . . from retreat. Their food running out, their wounded suffering. . . .

Toward mid-afternoon, they reached regimental headquarters at a little village called Wesu Ga, on a river. The noise of battle seemed only a half-mile away. As they marched in, Jerry gaped at the bustle—the constant coming and going of soldiers, and pack mules loaded with ammunition. A telephone line had been strung out into the jungle and in a rice paddy a radio antenna had been run up like an insect's feeler. Two soldiers were operating the hand-cranked transmitter beneath it. A heavy-weapons platoon was ready to move out, and from a *basha* in the village couriers came and went at a trot. On the edge of the river, in foxholes, several hundred Marauders of the First Battalion were waiting to be ordered into battle.

Jerry left the demolitions platoon and walked into the village to ask the way to Second Battalion. In the shade between two huts was an aid station where wounded men were being cared for. They lay on blankets, their helmets beside them. Rifles, thrust bayonet-down into the earth, served as uprights to support bottles of plasma. Under a shelter of ponchos stretched between the huts, a team of surgeons were operating on the badly wounded. A chaplain was taking a letter from one of the men lying on a blanket.

Jerry had a desire to look over the weary, bloody faces in the aid station to see whether Russ or Ben or any of the others from his platoon were there, but he hurried on to what looked like a company headquarters. As he neared the *basha*, a sentry with a Tommy gun suddenly challenged him, his unshaven features sharp with warning.

"All right—hold it there!" he snapped, leveling the gun.

Jerry had never seen him before. Startled, he said quickly, "Corporal Harada—I & R platoon, Second Battalion."

"What are you doing here, if you're with Second?"

An officer on the porch of the hut glanced down.

"I've been on detached service in Delhi. I just came in with a pioneer and demolition bunch from command headquarters."

"Let's see your special orders," the officer said, starting down the steps. He was young, but looked drawn and tired.

"Wait, Captain!" the guard warned. "He may have a canteen full of high explosives, for all we know. All I know is he's a Jap."

The captain went on, however, keeping out of line so that the soldier could hose Jerry with his Tommy gun if it became necessary.

"My orders are in my shirt pocket," Jerry said. "Shall I get them out?" At a gesture from the officer, he drew them out. The officer read them quickly. In the background was the incessant, roaring undertone of battle.

"All right," the officer said, returning them. "I'll send a man to get you started. The password's 'Eclipse.' "

"What's—what's going on, sir?" Jerry asked, tucking the paper away.

"We've set blocks north and south on the road. Second's trying to keep the northern block in. Third's having its troubles with the southern. The Japs are going crazy because they can't get through."

Then his face tensed; he glanced up at the sky sharply. A silken *whew-whew-whew!* was approaching from the south, an ominous whistling. Along the village street he saw soldiers throwing themselves flat.

On the porch of the headquarters hut, the guard bawled, "Big one, Captain—duck!"

The whistling ended suddenly.

Jerry saw the officer dive for the ground, his hands over his ears. Jerry was too stunned to move. Everyone else seemed to be sprawling on the ground or under a *basha*. An instant after the whistling died, there was a mighty *blam!* which shook the ground. Mud and smoke erupted at the end of the street. With a twist of sickness, Jerry saw what he was sure was part of a human body flying high in the air.

All at once he shivered and began to react. He fell to the ground, his ears humming. A few seconds later there was a second whistling through the sky, an instant of silence, and then a mighty explosion. The report, this time, was farther off.

Now Jerry could hear a man bawling, "Medic! *Medic!*"

Men were running from the aid station down the street, each of them carrying a folded litter under his arm.

The officer stood up. "Just a stray," he said. "They're zeroing in on a target someplace near us, though. We'll probably have to pull out of here before morning. Okay," he said briskly, "do you know where Second Battalion headquarters is?"

"No, sir. I don't even know where Second is."

"Cross the river on the stakes. Headquarters is between the river and the road, just off the trail. Remember that password?"

"Eclipse."

"Be ready with it. Better let 'em see you're a Nisei, too, not a Jap. Feeling's running high out there. Tanaka seems to be moving in a couple of regiments to throw at us. Okay —take off, Corporal."

Jerry turned and hurried down the street to the edge of the rice paddy. It was here that the shell had landed. Out in the soft earth a huge crater had been blasted. It was oozing smoke like a volcano. All about were the foxholes of the waiting troops. Two medics were kneeling by a man near the smoking margin of the crater.

Jerry trotted toward the river, found some stakes at the edge of it with bits of red cloth tied to them, and across the river saw other stakes. He waded into the water, holding his rifle high. He emerged soaked to the waist, and went on into the jungle.

On both sides of the trail, the jungle crowded in with its massive green shadows, darker still as dusk settled over the valley. He wanted to run—to find someone to share his fears with. But where he was going the crashing, rattling uproar of battle was much louder; he did not expect to find much comfort when he arrived. Muscles were trying to cramp in his chest, and his palms slipped greasily on his rifle.

In all his life he had never been so tired. His boots were like stones; his pack crushed him down, and he felt pain in his recently healed wound. At every turn in the trail he halted and fought with himself before he could make himself pass it, because it was at the turns that things happened. The *whew-whew-BLAM!* of shelling was incessant.

At last he came to a turn where a number of Marauders occupied a strong point. The trampled earth showed that many men had left the trail here to enter the jungle. He gave the countersign and was passed, and a few minutes later he came into the feverish activity of the command post, a big clearing in the forest.

The firing was terrifyingly close, shaking the leaves and branches. There were a lot of men around, most of them in foxholes, and a great many officers coming and going. A telephone wire ran up into the trees. Medics were coming in with dead and wounded on litters, and a few of the walking wounded moved painfully toward the aid station on bamboo crutches, or supporting one another.

Jerry asked a runner who was hurrying away with a message, "Where's I & R platoon, buddy?"

"Which team?" The man looked feverish and exhausted.

"Huh?" Jerry said—and saw the soldier's face harden as he looked at Jerry's Oriental features and then began to swing his carbine from its sling over his shoulder. Jerry talked fast. "I left on detached duty from Deogarh before this team business came up, I guess. I'm in I & R—Second Battalion."

The Marauder relaxed. "Well, there's two combat teams—Blue and Green. Supposed to be a couple of Niseis on each. I'll take you to Green—I think they're short a man. Got any water in your canteen? We've been dry all day."

Jerry gave him a drink, and the runner led him to a sort of alcove in the jungle off the main clearing. In a foxhole, Lieutenant Grissom, the I & R officer, was talking over a walkie-talkie. "I can't read you, Bennett—I can't read you!" he said desperately. "Can you talk louder?"

Jerry felt a weakness in the knees. Somewhere at the end of that wire Russ was talking to the lieutenant. In all this hell of artillery bombardment, he was still alive.

Grissom said again, "You'd better come on in! We're pulling in the perimeter for the night. Roger," he said, and hung up. Then he laid his arm on the parapet of the trench and rested his head against it, exhausted.

"Lieutenant?" Jerry said. The lieutenant raised his head and looked around. He was sick—that was obvious. Most of the men, Jerry had learned, were suffering from malaria and dysentery.

"Yes?" Grissom said.

"Corporal Harada," Jerry said. "I've been on detached duty in Delhi, sir. I had orders—"

"Have you got any water?"

Jerry uncapped his canteen and the officer drank a little of it. "Sir, isn't the trail open to the river?" Jerry asked.

Grissom stared at him. "Don't tell me you just came down it! It's been open and closed like a Boy Scout knife all day!"

Jerry swallowed. "I guess it was open when I came through. . . ."

"Dig yourself a hole and crawl into it. They haven't shelled us yet, but they're bound to start eventually. The battalion's been catching hell for two days. If we just had a few pieces of artillery to hand it back to them—!"

Jerry unloaded his pack near the edge of the clearing and began digging with his entrenching tool. Shells were still whistling over. He had the goose-fleshy feeling that at any moment one of those shells was going to land on him.

CHAPTER 21

# The Line

The artillery barrage slackened after dark, but the flash of the closer bursts could be seen reflected against the smoke drifting above the trees. Russ slumped in the foxhole he had dug near Jerry's. Jerry had hardly known him. He had not shaved in three weeks, and his cheeks and eyes looked sunken. Sprawling there, he shivered with a sudden malarial chill.

"Had yours yet?" he asked.

"Not yet. I've been moving too fast for the mosquitoes to catch me." A shell crashed into the jungle near them, and they both ducked. Jerry raised his head. "Doesn't this ever stop?"

"It hasn't for two days. Everybody on the line has the shakes. I saw a big sergeant crying like a baby, shaking so he couldn't handle his machine gun. He swore he wasn't scared—he just couldn't stop shaking."

"What's happening?" Jerry asked. "Where *is* this line people talk about?"

"I don't know. Nobody knows. For twenty-four hours after we made contact with the enemy, we just tore around the jungle running into each other and having little skirmishes. It started after we blocked the road here and down the line a couple of miles. They'd pulled out of their foxholes that night, and we moved into them. In the morning we ambushed a couple of trucks heading up the road when they came back—and then it really started! They made six attacks that day—every one of them a real banzai. By that night they'd lost over a hundred dead!"

"How many did we lose?" Jerry asked.

"Five and one—five wounded, one killed," Russ said. He shoved a cleaning patch down the barrel of his rifle, shaking his head as he rammed it back and forth. "They fight like they were crazy! I saw fifteen men attack a machine-gun nest, five at a time—and not a man got to it. The first wave went down and the second climbed over them—and went down too. The third wave crawled over the first ten and died on top of them. They're still lying there in the road. But there seem to be hundreds more to replace the ones they lose."

"What happens to the wounded?" Jerry asked, picturing the scene more vividly than he liked.

"They leave most of theirs. We've got all ours back so far. Sometimes the medics or a man's buddies have to go out under fire to carry a wounded man in. We've settled down to more or less stable lines, now, except that every so often a few of them infiltrate behind us. We've been cut off from the regiment twice today!"

"What's I & R doing?"

"Interpreting their battle orders, written and verbal—

they do a lot of shouting during an attack. That way we usually know where they're going to hit next. This afternoon we've been out hunting their main telephone line. They must have one, but we can't find it." Russ laid the cleaning rod aside and lay back. He was still shivering.

"You'd better get some sleep," Jerry told him.

"Yeah, I guess," Russ muttered, and a few moments later Jerry saw his jaw sagging and knew he was asleep.

About midnight the artillery almost ceased. Jerry fell asleep, though every few moments he would wake with a start. It was like falling asleep in a chair and imagining it was tipping over. While it was still dark, Lieutenant Grissom wakened him. Jerry started up, then relaxed and listened to the lieutenant's steady, low voice.

"Harada, you're going out with Sugeta and Matsumoto to look for their telephone line."

"Yes, sir."

"I think dawn may be the safest time for it, because their big daily attack comes then. The Japs will be too busy with us to patrol the line. Sugeta knows where we've looked and where we haven't. Try to avoid contact with the enemy. We're short enough of linguists without our Niseis getting shot up."

"I'll do all I can to make the supply last, sir," Jerry said with a feeble smile.

"Sugeta will have a Tommy gun for you. I'll turn your carbine in."

Sugeta and Matsumoto came to pick him up while he

was eating a breakfast of field rations. He had no appetite, but ate to keep his strength up. His stomach seemed to be full of flying insects, and he kept yawning, as he used to in school before he had to make a speech. Though the morning was oppressively warm, his hands were chilled.

"Let's go," Ben said. He laid a battered submachine gun at the rim of Jerry's foxhole, with six long clips of ammunition in a canvas belt. As he loaded the gun, Jerry looked at Ben. He was wearing a long-sleeved olive drab undershirt from which he had cut the sleeves. His belt was decorated with hand grenades, and he carried a Tommy gun with the stock removed for lightness.

As he checked the loads of his gun, Jerry asked, "What happened to that hand-carved rifle, Ben?"

Ben grimaced. "It was bad luck. I traded it to a mule-skinner who liked the hearts I carved on it. He carved his own initials and his girl's on them. Then the poor guy got wounded. Some other guy got the gun after they flew him out—and he got a piece of shrapnel in the chest! Guess I got rid of it just in time."

"Better show Jerry where we're going," Matsumoto grunted. He had become very sober since Jerry saw him last. He seemed grave and preoccupied.

On a message pad, Ben drew a little map showing regimental headquarters, the village of Lagang Ga, and another village called Walawbum, farther down. Then he made an X to show where they were now. The map made a terribly complex situation look very clear.

"It's not as simple as it looks," Ben admitted, "because we may go ten feet and run into a Jap in the bushes! One of them nearly got General Merrill yesterday right at regimental headquarters! But I guess we still control the road between Walawbum and where it crosses the Nambyu River. We're going farther west of the river today to look for that telephone line again."

"Is Russ going along?"

"No. He's up on the perimeter listening in on their commands."

As they went out, the uproar of artillery suddenly rose with a shattering crescendo. Jerry stopped for an instant, startled, but Matsumoto gave him a nudge from behind. He hurried on. The trail through the jungle was narrow. As they neared the road, they could hear the heavy crash of big artillery shells landing, and the steady slam of smaller pieces. There seemed to be only an instant's delay between the roar of the cannon and the explosion of the projectile; the firing rate was unbelievably rapid. The gun, he learned from Ben, was a Japanese Whiz-bang, a terrible morale-breaker. It kept the troops pinned down in their foxholes and the incessant explosions and stinging rains of shrapnel were worse than machine-gun fire.

Sugeta glanced back, his face sweaty and taut. "On your toes! We're almost to the road."

The firing was now at their left. They were a half-mile up the road from the roadblock where the battle was taking place. There were fewer trees here, but it only meant that the jungle growth was denser. When Sugeta halted, Jerry could hardly believe the road was just ahead. But after Ben moved up a few feet more he got a glimpse of a wide trail through the jungle. Ben lay down, and Jerry and Matsumoto followed. From the wet, big-leaved thicket, they peered down the road. The tracks of many vehicles had corrugated it deeply. They searched the road and the few trees for enemy snipers or patrols. The beating of Jerry's heart vibrated his whole body. He was aware of mosquitoes humming in the stillness, and when one landed on his hand he slapped it. The sound was startlingly loud. Both Ben and Matsumoto frowned at him.

At Ben's signal, they rose and stole at a crouch onto the road. For about a hundred feet in both directions the road was visible. Crossing quickly, they re-entered the thickets and burrowed into them gratefully. As they went on, Jerry began searching overhead for the glint of a copper wire. There were few trees, and he began to realize something: if the line followed the road, it would have to be visible somewhere in this stretch as it made its long swings between the trees. Perhaps that was why Sugeta had brought them here. Suddenly he saw a gleam of metal in one of the trees. He raised his Tommy gun, fearing a sniper. But Sugeta, who had seen it too, whispered: "There it is!"

Even so, he did not hurry. They moved cautiously. The wire was strung across a little meadow of tall elephant grass dotted here and there with trees. They threaded a narrow animal-trail to the base of one of the tall trees, and gazed up at a wire fixed to a green insulator just below the first branch.

"Go on up—you've got the instrument," Sugeta told Matsumoto.

The tree was slender enough to be climbed like a telephone pole. Matsumoto shinnied up it, reached the lateral branch, and got seated. Then he unlimbered a small sack he carried and removed some wires and a telephone receiver. He made a connection to the wire and put the receiver to his ear. Immediately his face lighted up.

"It's operating!" he signaled.

For a while he listened. Then he began writing on a message pad. He hesitated, frowned, and crumpled the sheet.

"What's the matter?" Sugeta called.

"It's clear, but I can't follow their lingo. I guess it's some kind of code—"

"What are they talking about?"

"Well, it seems to be a supply sergeant asking for something. I got the location."

"Come on down. Let me try."

Matsumoto dropped his message pad and they studied the map he had made. A big X had been marked beside the Nambyu River, above Walawbum. As soon as the Nisei had descended, Ben shinnied up. He spoke poor English, but his Japanese was as slangy as anyone could desire. He had not listened in long when he began writing fast. He started dropping slips of paper with Japanese words scrawled on them, a few words to each page. Matsumoto rapidly translated Sugeta's basic Japanese to good English.

"*. . . Urgently request support. . . . Ammunition dump close to Second Battalion m.l.r. . . . Only three riflemen to protect it. . . . Must emphasize again terribly dangerous situation. . . .*"

Matsumoto finished and handed the message to Jerry. "On the run, kiddo," he said hastily.

"Where to—the C.P.?"

"That's right. You wanted to be an I & R man, didn't you?" Matsumoto grinned.

Jerry put the slip in the pocket of his fatigue jacket and started off. He moved fast, aware that the message he carried might have great significance. He hoped he could remember the way. . . .

Lieutenant Grissom was exultant when he read the message. "So their amo dump's in trouble. Great! Maybe we can send help in the form of a dive bomber. Take off, Corporal. Keep us posted."

As he was returning, Jerry heard voices at the road. He lay in the bushes, shivering with excitement. After a moment he saw movement: across the road, three Japanese soldiers were setting up a machine gun behind a screen of leaves. Jerry felt as though he were suffocating—his heart filled his whole chest with its explosive hammering. He watched the men in their pot-helmets and wrap-leggings working feverishly, bracing the gun carriage and feeding a tape of ammunition into the breech.

They gave no evidence of being part of a larger group, paying no attention to the road above or below; they seemed in a great rush to get the machine gun into position. Jerry tried to picture exactly how he must proceed. Carefully he took a hand grenade from his belt and pulled the pin. He let the lever snap up, heard the fuse begin to sizzle, and tossed it across the road. As it landed in the bushes, one of the men straightened quickly.

"What was that?" he called excitedly.

Jerry lay flat. The grenade exploded with a sharp crash. Shrapnel whistled over his head. He raised himself and saw one man down and another holding his bleeding wrist. The third was holding an automatic weapon ready to fire, but he did not know in which direction to fire it. Jerry raised his Tommy gun and pushed it through the trees. It had seemed terrible, that night with the Kachins, to send a carbine bullet crashing into a man's body. All that bothered him now was getting the Japanese before they got him.

He squeezed the trigger.

The gun jumped in his hand, its muzzle rising irresistibly. Forcing it down, he gave another burst and saw both Japanese sink to the ground. He waited. Bitter and gray, the smoke drifted across the road. The soldiers lay on their backs.

From up the road, no sound came; from down it, nothing. He ran across the road to the path and plunged with relief into the jungle.

"What was the racket?" Matsumoto asked him when he returned.

Jerry put his little finger in the muzzle of the gun and twisted it. He showed the powder grime, and Matsumoto stared. "Kiddo, you're learning," he said.

Not long after, the roar of a dive bomber was heard. They looked up and saw a plane dropping from the sky almost vertically into the jungle. It pulled up sharply, climbed and disappeared, but in a few minutes it was back. This time it dropped at a steep angle toward a point south of the telephone line. They could see its guns blazing. At the last instant before it dropped from sight, it pulled into a steep climb, a bomb shaking loose from each wing.

They heard the *crump* of the exploding bombs. Then a massive, shattering roar tore the air so that the leaves trembled. A column of dense black smoke began to mount into the sky. The Niseis looked at one another almost guiltily. They knew that "support" had been brought to the ammunition dump in the form of two bombs. . . .

All that day they monitored the telephone line, taking turns at carrying the messages. ". . . *Casualties very large, we cannot protect river crossing. . . . Enemy very strong. . . . Cannot hold much longer if help does not come. . . .*"

The Japs were having their troubles, too, it appeared.

An hour before sundown, a message was intercepted

from Tanaka's headquarters ordering the Eighteenth Division to withdraw. It was now too late to remain any longer at the telephone line. They all had a strong feeling that they had played their luck to the end, and they returned hurriedly to headquarters. Here preparations were being made to pull back across the river as soon as possible. The battalion had been without water for thirty-six hours and was now out of food. The Chinese, according to reports, were forcing their way down the road and by tomorrow night would occupy the position in strength. But in the meantime a localized attack in great strength was feared.

In the black night the battalion withdrew, carrying their wounded on litters. Despite the message that Tanaka was pulling the Eighteenth south, there were frightening rumors that hordes of Japanese infantry had come up the road by truck and were about to attack. It was the sort of fear to which sick, overwrought soldiers were prey. Jerry knew first-hand how it was with sick soldiers: during the last few hours on the telephone line, he had begun to shake with fever.

CHAPTER 22

# Task Force!

The regiment pulled back as the Chinese forces came up. With the Chinese came artillery, and soon they began to hear the cheerful hammering of it as they occupied the positions the Marauders had just pulled out of. It began to look to the Americans as though they were running interference for a Chinese backfield.

For two days they rested at Shikau Ga, eating, swimming and sunning themselves.

They absorbed the startling figures that eight hundred Japanese had been killed in five days, against only eight Marauders killed and thirty-seven wounded. It sounded so simple. In reality, most of the Japanese losses had been incurred in their suicidal charges against the Third Battalion, dug in above the river, and against Second in their initial charge after the block was set on the road.

But seventy other Marauders had been evacuated with sickness and combat fatigue. The outfit was beginning to slow down. Jerry's initial attack of chills and fever relaxed its enervating grip. He had been dosed with various medicines, but the rest and food did the most good. Nearly all the men were down with fever, and many had big, ugly Naga sores on their legs, where mites had dug in and infected the flesh. On some, the flesh had wasted away clear to the shinbone.

But the recreation time was about up—they knew it when briefing talks were held for the officers. After one talk, Lieutenant Grissom displayed a map to the I & R platoon showing where they were heading next, the village of Shaduzup, on down the road.

The Marauders were impressed by their own progress. General Stilwell said they had forced the Japanese back farther in three days than the Chinese had forced them in the preceding three months. They were driving a hard, slanting blow at the Japanese army. With luck, said the lieutenant, they would take Kamaing before the monsoon.

"Before the monsoon!" The phrase was heard more and more. The monsoon was the rainy season, lasting from April to October. "We'll set the Japs back on their heels before the monsoon," Grissom predicted. They would have to. For when the skies opened above Burma, the land would drown for six months. Air operations would end, blinded by fog and cloud. The earth would swell like a sponge. Anopheles and several other malaria mosquitoes would breed in singing, deadly clouds, and fevers would begin their annual toll of thousands of lives.

The Marauders had been promised they would be flown out before the monsoon. But there was mounting uneasiness that they had fought too well: Stilwell's Northern Combat Area Command, exhilarated by the strength and speed of Operation Galahad, might decide to press for the important airfield of Myitkyina, "Mitch," to the foot soldier.

Coming from a final briefing, Lieutenant Grissom growled, "What do they think we are—pack mules? *Now* they're talking about heading across the mountains to Mitch, after we take Shaduzup!" He pointed to a village on the map. It was near the foot of the Burma Road—over a hundred miles away!

Meanwhile they were suddenly packing for the march to Shaduzup, at the foot of the Hukawng Valley.

What headquarters had in mind was another wide, flanking sweep around left end, then a swift doubling-back to smash at Shaduzup. Shaduzup was a strong point on the Kamaing Road.

When the hour came to push south, the Marauders learned that the outfit was being split up. They had a superstitious feeling that it was a dangerous move. There was an old military maxim that you should never divide your forces. Nevertheless, for this strike, First Battalion would forge south across the Jambu Bum Hills, then cut west to cut the road at Shaduzup. Second and Third were to parallel First's line of march farther east, but would march fifteen miles farther south before they also turned west to try to block the road.

The march started.

For five days, Second and Third followed a beautiful

river gorge. Jerry was too tired and feverish to enjoy the magnificent scenery. He was realizing that proving one's courage was not so simple a matter as getting up and volunteering for hazardous service: it was a long and wearing battle.

From the river, the long column wound snakelike to a ridge dividing two valleys. They looked down on cloud-filled steamy canyons. Then for another eight days they marched through forests and village clearings along the spine of the mountains. The big Hukawng Valley was behind them, now, but ahead, spreading south and west, was the Mogaung Valley, lumpy and green with forest and jungle. Down the near edge of the valley ran the Kamaing Road. They had almost come in striking distance of Inkangatawng, where they would attack.

A radio message came from Stilwell. "*Japs withdrawing down Road. Shaduzup fell today. Come fast!*" They knew, now, that First Battalion had succeeded in its part of the mission and would soon start south to join them.

"Come fast!" the officers groaned.

They had thought they were already coming fast! But the pace of the march was mercilessly quickened, while along with the increased speed came occasional downpours of rain. Under the green ponchos covering them, the men looked humpbacked. The mules slid in the mud and a few went over the steep trailside and were lost.

Then they left the ridge trail, and in two days dropped

thousands of feet to the edge of the valley. As they moved toward the road, security orders went up and down the line: ". . . Five yard intervals! . . . No talking. . . ."

They were in flat jungle again. They reached a broad river and made the crossing unobserved. Inkangatawng was only a half-mile ahead. "Weapons platoon forward!" the order was passed back. Marching at the point, the reconnaissance platoon experienced the familiar cramping of muscles, the terrible suspense, the jerking of nerves as someone stepped on a dry branch. Then there was a shattering paralysis of shock as gunfire lashed at them from the jungle.

A wounded man screamed. There was a great rustle as the column got into position. "Medics forward!" the cry came.

Experience began to show in their reactions. Scouts left the trail to grope for the enemy, testing his strength with cautious jabs. From here and there could be heard the soft rattle of Japanese weapons, the harsher clatter of American fire. The main force waited, while patrols went out to try to surround the village. But, from the sound of the heavy firing, the column knew they were running into strong opposition, and uneasiness came with the darkness. They heard the roar of trucks on the road. Artillery coming up! Truckloads of artillery and heavy weapons companies!

Then a Japanese radio message was intercepted which threw the whole operation in jeopardy. A Japanese task force was moving up from the south. Its mission: to drive on to

Shaduzup and retake the village First Battalion had just won!

Several thousand men were in the task force, which was moving up the same trail the Marauders had just left to descend to the valley. If this force was not blocked, all the gains the Americans had made so far might be lost, and the regiment itself would be marooned.

General Merrill did the only thing there was to do. He ordered Second and Third back up to the ridge to try to intercept the Japanese.

At dawn, all units were pulled back from Inkangatawng and the retreat up the steep trail they had just come down was started. On the maps, a little village called Nhpum Ga had been marked as the spot where they would dig in and wait for the Japanese—unless the Japanese beat them there. Third Battalion led the way back up the mountain trail, with Second slipping and sliding in the greasy mud behind them. All night clouds had been massing, and now a tropical downpour descended. Gazing up the steep, winding trail as Second started painfully back to the ridge, Jerry wondered whether he could make it, whether any of them could make it. Two days down—how many up? He was sick, shaking with fever, his joints aching. The men ahead of him staggered along; he followed them. They had wounded to carry after the night's skirmishing. Four men at the head of a platoon would carry a litter for fifteen or twenty minutes; when they were too tired to continue, the litter was passed back to the next four. Now and then a litter-bearer would slip in the mud and go to his knees; the wounded man would cry out. In his misery and desperation, Jerry knew that of all the terrible things which could befall a man, war was the worst.

They marched until after dark, but were still short of the ridge. From where they bivouacked in the rain, they could see lights flashing and a few fires some distance south. It was clear then that if they beat the Japanese to Nhpum Ga, it would be by a few scant hours.

In the morning they made the ridge—and ran into an artillery barrage.

The enemy had moved pack howitzers into position during the night. Artillery spotters directed a savage fire all along the ridge where the trail was exposed. Pack animals were going down and every now and then an exhausted foot soldier would fall with a shrapnel wound. Medics cut holes in their litters to let the rain water escape. A few men who were killed outright were hastily buried, and the column struggled on through the rain and the shelling.

Word came back that Third had passed through Nhpum Ga and occupied the village of Hsamsingyang a few miles beyond it. The rain let up; the land steamed. Clouds filled the valleys, but behind them, coming fast, Second Battalion saw the Japanese closing in. "Speed it up!" the command came down the column.

At ten-thirty in the morning, Second reached the divide where the tiny village of Nhpum Ga straddled two valleys. They began at once to dig in. Within an hour, the battle of Nhpum Ga commenced. It was not to end for eleven days.

# CHAPTER 23

# Battle of Nhpum Ga

Through the battalion a question ran endlessly, like an invalid's complaint: *Why don't we keep moving?* They were ahead of the task force: By forced marches they could make it to safety at Shaduzup, joining First Battalion and whatever Chinese troops had been moved in to occupy the roadblock set by First. But Second Battalion knew the answer to the question: they had to prevent the task force from marching north and enveloping First and the Chinese. At all costs, they had to make it too expensive for the Japanese to pass.

Through that morning, stragglers kept floundering into the village of four or five *bashas* around which defenses were being dug with panicky haste. The skies had cleared; the sun scorched the sodden jungle. A mule which had died of wounds began to bloat in a few hours. Medical aid stations were placed in sheltered areas, while along the quarter-mile strip of ridge straddling two valleys, gun emplacements were dug, mortars zeroed in on the approaches to the village, and automatic weapons placed. An aerial was run up; the big AN-PRC-1 radio started groping across the miles for contact with headquarters.

There was a feeling that the worst things which war had

to offer were about to be hurled at Second. Feverish and exhausted, the Marauders waited.

With his foxhole half-dug, Jerry, played out, sat on the ground, dull-eyed, gazing out over the valleys and rivers lying at the foot of the mountains. "Napoonga," as the Kachins pronounced the name of the village, rested in a high pass between valleys on the east and west. The road ran north and south. Five miles farther north was the village of Hsamsingyang, where Third Battalion was dug in. It was planned to keep the trail open between the battalions for the exchange of wounded and supplies.

A young rifleman came up to Jerry and almost shyly touched his arm. He had just come up the trail from the outfit's single water hole. He was not wearing his helmet, and his blond hair, long uncut, was ragged. The boy's face was full of awe.

"Corp'ral, I just seen a big plane land down there!" he whispered.

"A plane! You mean one crashed?"

"No, sir! A great big C-47! I think maybe it's carrying artillery for us. Or a hot meal—you 'member they promised us a hot meal after Inkangatawng?"

Jerry regarded him closely. "Where is the plane?"

The soldier led him to where the ridge dropped off sharply above a dense bamboo thicket. "There!"

Jerry searched the white-tasseled grove of bamboo on the almost vertical mountainside. "You mean it crashed in that?"

"No, sir! Right yonder—in the bamboo, see it? It's in a little clearin'."

"Oh, yes," Jerry said. "I see it now. The pilot's already hiking up the hill, isn't he? I'll tell you what—let's tell Major Rogoff, the medical officer, in case he wants to send out any wounded when the plane leaves again. Come on!"

At the aid station, a small number of men were digging slit trenches in which to lay the wounded. Already a few men who had been wounded earlier were lying in the trenches, while shelters of bamboo were erected to shade them from the harsh tropical sun. Major Rogoff was opening a crate of medical supplies in the surgery shelter.

"Major," Jerry said, "this man just spotted a C-47 down the hill. It landed in the bamboo." The major turned his head quickly to stare at him. "We thought," Jerry added, "you might want to evacuate some of the wounded when it leaves. . . ."

The major continued staring at him in disbelief. Then he understood. He smiled at the young soldier. "Sure enough. We'll certainly do that. In the meantime, soldier, will you give us a hand here? We're digging trenches for the wounded. You look rugged enough to help."

Pleased, the Marauder leaned his rifle against some crates. "Yes, sir, I'll be pleased to help, Major. Whereat do I start?"

The major turned him over to a staff sergeant who was supervising the work, and told Jerry quietly, "Any other psychos you see, send them up here. We need trenches, and they need their minds occupied. I've sent three of them back to the lines already!"

Second Battalion was dug in and ready. Late in the afternoon the rear guard, a mile south, had to pull back into the village. Artillery shells began winging in and the explosions threw up geysers of dirt. A few hours later, the first savage infantry charge smashed at the perimeter.

The fumbling, exhausted Marauders spelled each other through the night. Just at dawn the Japanese launched a screaming banzai attack. A sword-waving officer led his troops inside the American line before machine-gun fire broke his saber and dropped him. The Japanese piled up before the machine-gun emplacements, fighting to the last breath and screaming their battle cry—"Banzai!" meaning "May the Emperor live ten thousand years!" Actually, it was a talisman to evoke the last drop of courage from a fighting man. The attack lasted an hour before it was broken.

During the day, the water hole was lost; a few hours later the connecting trail to Third Battalion was cut. From the ridge, it was apparent that Third, in her snug valley, would be unable to help—she was having all she could do to prevent being surrounded herself. Second was on her own, now, and the men suffered a terrible loneliness. It was as though they had been at the end of a long, long rope, the other end of which was anchored at home. Now the rope had been cut.

The second morning brought another vicious bayonet attack. Automatic weapons hurriedly carried into position repelled it. Late in the day the water shortage began to be felt. There was not even enough water for the wounded to wash down their sulfa pills, nor to make plaster casts for shattered limbs. Jerry and some other men volunteered to work down to a spring to fill water bags. They were almost back when a Nambu opened up on them. One of Jerry's water bags was shot full of holes.

As dusk settled in, reddening the powder smoke which choked the ridge, the firing line was pulled back for security. They could hear the Japanese in their foxholes calling back and forth. They laughed a good deal; apparently they were confident of victory.

"I wonder what those guys talk about," Matsumoto grumbled. "They sound like they were having a party down there." He sniffed. "Smells like they're having turkey for dinner!"

"They are," Jerry said bitterly. "They got all of our last supply drop! Turkey for them—powdered eggs for us."

Now that it was darker, a man could look over the rim of his foxhole without being shot at. He gazed down the strip of no man's land between their main line of resistance and the Japanese positions. Dead mules, dead Japanese, shell craters, and ripped shrubbery made the area look like the aftermath of a hurricane. The chattering went on, just audibly enough to whet Jerry's curiosity.

A man wriggled close to his foxhole and Jerry glanced around. It was Lieutenant Grissom. "Everything okay?" he asked.

"Okay, Lieutenant," Jerry said.

Grissom listened to the careless talk and laughter from the Japanese lines. "Can you make out any of it?" he asked.

"Not from here," Jerry said. Then he looked across at Matsumoto. He could tell from the Nisei's silence that his thoughts paralled Jerry's. "What do you think, Roy?"

"I think so too," Roy sighed.

"We'd better let it get good and dark before we leave," Jerry said.

So without anyone's openly mentioning it, the plan came into being. They would crawl down into the enemy line and listen in on the conversations.

"I wouldn't ask anyone to take the risk," said Grissom. "But if we could get a lead on where they're going to hit us tomorrow morning, we might be able to move some automatic weapons there and be ready for them."

Gazing across the torn ground, Jerry felt goose-flesh ripple up his arms. The slightest sound at night invariably brought heavy fire from a dozen points. And what if they got through?—could they possibly lie near enough to the foxholes to listen in without being seen? But this was what they had volunteered for—to do jobs other men could not.

"What will the password be, sir?" Jerry asked.

"Lillian," said Grissom. "The countersign is Russell."

From another foxhole, Sugeta spoke almost sleepily.

Dengue fever had racked him the last few days, the brutal, enervating "breakbone fever." "We can't take rifles," he said. "What about automatics, Lieutenant?"

"I'll round up three forty-fives for you," the officer said.

After dark the firing died down. Sporadically an automatic weapon would open up when a noise was heard in the narrow strip between the lines, or a grenade would split the darkness with a sharp cracking explosion and a burst of light. A man trying to cover a dead mule with gravelly earth would bring a dozen stuttering explosions of machine-gun fire before he finished. The stench from dead animals was becoming so unbearable, the mantle of black flies so terrible, that repeated attempts were made to bury them.

At nine o'clock, the jungle darkness complete, the Niseis prepared to leave. Each man carried an automatic pistol and a few grenades. Matsumoto and Sugeta were to crawl down the western face of the ridge at two different points. Jerry would slip into the bamboo thicket on the eastern perimeter.

He crawled from the platoon command post to a machine-gun nest, whispering to the gunners, "I'll try to come back this way. "What's your password?"

"Lillian," one of the gunners said.

"Russell," Jerry said.

"Good luck," the gunner whispered.

Jerry crawled over the dry ground. He was grateful for the shell craters. But each crater made as good a hiding place for a Japanese as well as an American, and he always went in pistol-first. Before he had gone far, he could hear talking; a man laughed and there was a clink of metal. His stomach knotted; he was not over fifty feet from an enemy foxhole. Inch by inch, he went on. The darkness was so great the eyes never seemed to become accustomed to it. Reaching the edge of the bamboo, he settled into a crater to listen. He did not want to enter the thicket if he could avoid it; he was almost certain to make a sound.

In his breast his heart throbbed like a drum. Every vein in his body echoed it. He lay on his back to rest, gazing up at the brilliant stars. A man laughed. Jerry raised his head to listen.

"Remember the night before we left Singapore?" a voice said softly in Japanese. "I had a hangover for three days!"

"Three days! I've still got one," another man said.

"To think I had a chance to go in the air force," a third voice said after a pause. "What a blockhead I was to pass it up."

"I don't know—the kind of planes they're giving them to fly."

"You tell me anything that's worse than wading in mud!"

Silence for a while.

"I'll trade you some smoked fish for a rice cake," a man said.

"Not me. I'm saving this for a celebration."

"What's an infantryman got to celebrate?"

"Not being a medic."

The men chuckled. A man yawned. "I'm going to get some sleep."

Jerry lay there. Suddenly he heard a sound back toward his own lines. The Japanese heard it too, and a Nambu erupted instantly with a string of shots. They went ripping directly over his head.

"Simpleton," one of the Japanese said. "You're shooting at owls!"

"Maybe Yankee owls."

After this there was a long interval of silence. Both armies seemed to sleep. Jerry, too, was drowsy. He could feel the rim of his helmet cutting the back of his neck as he lay there. He was glad for the discomfort, for it kept him awake. At least he thought it would keep him awake. He came to full awareness with a start, automatically raising his pistol and staring around him in terror. The machine gun had ripped out a long burst. The voices were intense, now. He knew by the stars he had slept for a long time.

"It sounded like snoring, Akira."

"Yes—your own!"

"No—right out there in front!"

Jerry shuddered. It was his own snoring they had heard!

"Now, nobody's going to crawl down from Second Battalion to sleep in front of a machine-gun nest!"

After a long period of silence, the men seemed to accept the fact that it was a false alarm. With infinite pains, Jerry turned himself over.

"What time is it?"

"Quarter to four."

"Hey, we've got to move! C Company's jumping off in a half-hour."

Jerry could hear them stirring, collecting ammunition boxes and folding the trails of their machine gun. "I'm glad I'm going to be down here instead of going with the attack for a change," a soldier said. "Those rocks are crawling with machine guns."

"After the shelling we gave them yesterday? Dead guns, maybe."

The voices faded. Jerry turned and crept back to the lines. There was little time to prepare for the charge. He knew exactly the point they were discussing: the only rocks on the ridge were down the line a couple of hundred feet. He wriggled on, wanting to run but not daring even to crawl.

At last he knew he was close to the perimeter. He whispered into the darkness, "Lillian!"

"Russell!" came the countersign.

One of the machine-gunners patted him on the back as he came in. "What's new, Tojo?"

"Plenty—they're punching at the rocks in a half hour!"

At the command post, Lieutenant Grissom listened to his report. He said quickly, "Get some rest," and hurried away to discuss the information with the other officers.

Matsumoto came in a short time later. "Nothing," he said. "I could have heard the same chatter up here. Women and food."

Sugeta arrived shortly with information on the placement of a Whiz-bang cannon. By now there was a stirring up and down the line as heavy weapons were shifted to meet the attack. The sky was growing gray in the east.

Lieutenant Grissom returned, tense and excited. "You're sure of what you heard?"

"I didn't dream it, Lieutenant."

"I hope not. We're pulling the perimeter back and moving half the weapons platoon to cover the attack!"

"Pulling it *back?*" Jerry echoed.

"We're emptying the front-line foxholes and booby-trapping them. If they come, they'll think they've walked into a rifle range!"

# CHAPTER 24

# State of Siege

From Jerry's position, he could see the dark ground where the attack was expected to take place. The Japanese line was hidden by heavy growth. Before it stretched fifty yards of clear ground, then an area plowed by artillery and pocked with foxholes. In the midst of this section was a nest of boulders. They had been blasted repeatedly by artillery, so that it had been necessary to evacuate them. But the foxholes had been manned until this morning, when, in the darkness, the Marauders had crawled back to new positions closer to the village after booby-trapping their foxholes.

Jerry and Matsumoto occupied a shell-crater back from the edge of the now-deserted front-line pocket. A weak light began to seep through the sky. There were faint cries from the jungle. "Here they come!" Jerry whispered.

There were cries of "*Banzai!*" Grenades began falling in the newly evacuated area. The explosions were like the reports of cannon-crackers. Dark figures rushed from the jungle with bayonets gleaming. Jerry estimated there must be at least seventy-five soldiers advancing among the foxholes, thrusting their bayonets downward in savage thrusts.

Not an American weapon was fired.

The Japanese halted, confused. Then an officer waved his sword. "Death to the Americans!" he screamed. The Marauders let them come within fifty feet. Then every weapon opened up with a shocking din. Every man in the Japanese wave was cut down.

Almost immediately a second rush of soldiers came from the jungle. Another screaming charge commenced. Reaching the foxholes, the Japanese dropped into them for shelter from the machine guns now sweeping back and forth like fire hoses. Explosions were heard here and there as a booby trap exploded. Bodies were flung into the air. The soldiers who had not taken shelter dived into shell-craters and began firing back at the Marauders.

All at once Roy Matsumoto reared up and bawled, "*Susume! Susume!* Charge!"

Thinking it was one of their own officers shouting, the Japanese left their shelters and stumbled on into the raking fire. In the growing light, they could be seen falling everywhere. Jerry felt weak. A few soldiers wavered and started back; they too were shot down. The attack ended; the last BAR went silent. A morning breeze brushed the smoke aside; as the dawn strengthened the Marauders counted fifty-four dead. Jerry looked at Matsumoto. Matsumoto was looking at him. Both of them were numb.

"I was listening to some of those guys in C Company—the bunch we just cleaned out," Matsumoto murmured. "One of them was telling another about his little boy—

just three years old today. He was wishing he could send him a present. . . ."

"Let's get some sleep," Jerry said.

Matsumoto rubbed his rifle-stock. "You know, my mother lives in Japan," he said gloomily.

"Be glad she's not a soldier," Jerry tried to joke.

"No, I guess she's all right. She lives a long way from Tokyo—just a little city. I guess she's a lot safer than I am."

"Where does she live?" Jerry asked.

"Hiroshima," Matsumoto said.

So Second Battalion marked that day in red on its calendar of horror.

But it was clear now that no single loss was going to stop the Japanese. Their orders were to overrun the roadblock the Americans had set and hurry on to Shaduzup. They pried at the block with bayonets, artillery, and small arms. The Marauders threw them back day after day. Every night the Niseis went out and listened by the enemy foxholes; nearly every night they picked up information of value.

From the ridge, the besieged forces gazed enviously down on Third Battalion. Yet Third, secure in its little valley north of the ridge, was not enjoying its comparative safety. Patrols went out constantly to harass the Japanese. The trail to Nhpum Ga was slowly being reopened.

But when eight days had passed it became doubtful whether anything could happen in time to save Second from surrendering. Blood plasma was running out; there was no water but what could be squeezed out of clothing after a thundershower. A little hilltop near the village, which had hidden a nest of "fatboys"—eighty-one-millimeter mortars—had been blasted away completely by the never-ending artillery.

Then word came by radio that First Battalion was coming south by forced marches to break the siege. The Marauders dug in tighter and prayed harder. Encouraged by the hope of reinforcement, Third Battalion blasted back up the trail to within a half-mile of Nhpum Ga. Their two little howitzers lobbed shells across the ridge and down into the Japanese lines. Suddenly, on the tenth day, there was a sound of shouting which Second could hear over the rattle of small arms. What goes on? everyone wondered.

The answer came over the radio: First Battalion had arrived from Shaduzup!

From the jungle the sounds of patrol clashes grew heavier. First's men, though depleted from their forced march, were fanning out on both sides of the ridge in order to get in behind the enemy. One by one, the terrifying voices of the Whiz-bang cannons were stopped. Japanese machine guns stuttered and went silent.

At noon on the eleventh day of the siege—Easter Sunday— a Third Battalion patrol walked into the village. The siege was over.

Burial parties went out to dump enemy dead in foxholes and cover them. Mules, crawling with maggots and flies, were hosed with flame-throwers and laboriously covered with earth. A little cemetery of bamboo crosses was erected outside Nhpum Ga. Over a hundred wounded were carried down the trail to Hsamsingyang. New uniforms were handed out from bales dropped by air, and delicious field rations were passed out prodigally. The soldiers of Second Battalion began to look like men again.

But none of them would ever be the same men again, Jerry knew.

CHAPTER 25

# Rest and Recreation—Army Style

For a while it reminded Jerry of summer vacation.

There was plenty to eat. Cargo planes flew in every day to delight them with gaudy showers of colored parachutes—red, blue, and green—beneath which swung crates of hard goods, sacks of food, grain for the pack mules, and —to remind them they were not yet through—ammunition. They were free to hike down to the stream to bathe, wash clothing, and swim. Weapons which had been crusted with powder-grime and dirt were cleaned and oiled.

In his little steel pocket-mirror, Jerry scarcely recognized himself, for he had lost twenty-five pounds; but he could feel his body gathering itself to combat the foes that had invaded it—malaria and dengue, and the fierce Naga sores on his legs, just beginning to heal over. Yet there was one foe which none of the men seemed able to master: an overwhelming listlessness. They moved about like walking dead. Nothing was important enough to stir them.

All Jerry seemed to care about was a new relationship between himself and the Marauders, something better even than respect; perhaps it was admiration. The Marauders knew that without their language men they might never have survived the ordeal of Nhpum Ga. Niseis had discovered the presence of the task force they had just defeated. Had it been undiscovered, Second and Third Battalions would have been cut off and annihilated, First would have been enveloped at Shaduzup, and all the gains of the last month lost. Niseis had enabled them to anticipate the daily banzai attacks, had confused the Japanese with false orders over walkie-talkies. Colonel Hunter had thanked them in an order of the day, and it was known that several of the I & R boys were up for decorations after the end of the campaign.

One day Russ flopped down beside Jerry where he was washing his clothes in the river. "Heard the rumor?"

"I hear ten new ones a day."

"That we're being evacuated to Margherita for the rainy season. Six months, boy! Six months of solid rest!"

"I'll believe that when we get there."

"Okay, where *are* we going next?"

"I think we're going to dig in right here until November. Six months of solid rain and mud."

"You're a pessimist," Russ said.

Nevertheless there was something queer going on.

Staff officers were called to meetings from which they emerged thoughtful and worried. Once Jerry heard two of them talking as they left. What he heard made him uneasy. Later he was cleaning his gun with some of the other men.

Canvas buckets of soapy water rested between their feet.

"Where's Myitkyina?" he asked.

"Mitch?" said Russ, with a queer, sidelong glance. "Why?"

"Just curious."

"Southeast of here."

"What is it?" Jerry asked.

"A railroad and river town. It's the biggest Japanese supply center in northern Burma. Also it connects with the Burma Road."

"It's strategic, then?"

"You know it! If the rains weren't already starting, it would be our next mission. If we held Mitch and the big airfield there, we'd be able to reopen the Burma Road and supply China by truck again this year. But between us and Mitch there's a mountain range that's straight up and down. We'd never get over it, even in good weather."

Russ ran an oily cleaning patch through the barrel of his carbine. "Why all the interest in Mitch?"

"I heard Captain Senff and Colonel Beach talking about it this morning when they left the staff meeting. They looked pretty sick. The colonel was saying, 'We'd never get there, Tom!' "

The thrusting of cleaning rods and the scrubbing of old toothbrushes in the apertures of weapons ceased. "Cut it out!" Sugeta said gruffly. "Don't even joke about it!"

A state of shock settled in.

"Know what I think?" Jerry said. "We've done too good

a job. We've taken the Kamaing Road all the way from Maingkwan. We've set the clock ahead so far the planning department is thinking about opening the Burma Road before the rains!"

"*Before* the rains!" Matsumoto scoffed. "What did you think that was last night?"

Three inches of rain had fallen during the night, nearly washing the bivouac off the ridge. Jerry brooded.

"Remember how it was when you were a kid, and you could hardly keep your hands off the presents under the Christmas tree? That's the way it is with the big shots and Mitch—they can't keep their hands off it. They keep thinking, 'If we took Mitch, we'd have a big airfield in northern Burma—and a railroad town. And we'd be on a road that connects with the Burma Road!' "

They gazed at him, numbed. "We've got trucks rolling down the Kamaing Road all the way to Shaduzup, now," Jerry concluded. "If we took Mitch, they could roll all the way to China."

The silence gathered like smoke, but every man was thinking.

"What's the use talking about it?" Russ grunted, at last. "Even if we started, we'd never make it."

"I'll tell you one GI that's not even going to start," another man said. "Me! I'd get myself invalided out."

"Great!" someone else said. "How?"

"Stop taking my atabrine pills! My temperature would

go to a hundred and five in twenty-four hours. They'd have to evacuate me!"

"Oh, no they wouldn't," Jerry said. "They'd just court-martial you for not taking them."

So, because it was so impossible, the regiment regarded Myitkyina as a not-very-funny joke.

Rains sluiced down on the jungle, the earth turned to grease, the winds ripped the big leaves of the plants like paper. Then the sun came out and the land steamed. Mosquitoes appeared at dusk in such clouds that the men went about in nets like beekeepers. Still, the mosquitoes found their targets, and the malaria rate ascended.

Men were evacuated with blackwater fever, dengue, and combat fatigue. The incidence of heat exhaustion rose. Taking staunch Army steps against the alarming disease rate, the Army announced:

"It has been established that the taking of salt tablets in the prescribed manner will prevent heat exhaustion. Therefore, any man reporting on sick call with heat exhaustion will forfeit all pay and allowances until such time as he shall return to duty."

The Army could not discipline mosquitoes, however, and malaria continued to be the special plague of the 5307th. Meanwhile, the soldiers continued their normal bivouac duties:

They dug latrines and did KP.

They stood inspections.

They went out on patrols, some of which ended in brief, vicious clashes with the enemy.

They drilled with their special weapons.

And they wondered what would happen next. Until one day the suspense ended.

Sergeants gave the orders which resulted shortly in all the permanent-appearing canvas structures disappearing into packs on mule-backs and all personal soldier litter vanishing into sixty- and eighty-pound packs. All units fell in at a general formation. With no explanation, the regiment marched north again.

The column stretched out elastically, as the sick battalions straggled. Platoon leaders shouted at laggards and received the reply of angry, white-rimmed stares. The platoon leaders were too far gone to care. Mauled and feverish, the Marauders plodded along under their packs.

At Naubum two regiments of Chinese soldiers were waiting. The Marauders were bewildered. Standing in the rain, commanders explained what was about to take place.

"We are about to undertake Operation End Run. This will consist in crossing the Kumon Range, in whose foothills we now stand, and turning south to take the airfield of Myitkyina. Myitkyina is on the Irawaddy River and connects by secondary road with the Burma Road, farther south. We will not be required to take the town of Myitkyina itself. British and Chinese forces will relieve us as soon as the airfield has been secured. All personnel of the 5307th Composite Unit will then be evacuated for an extended period of rest and recuperation."

The final sentence was like a delicious dessert to end a tasteless meal. Rest and recuperation! Jerry looked up at the blue mountains soaring from the jungle. Beyond them were the incredible prizes of rest and recuperation. But could they get over those mountains? Driving mules over greasy trails, staggering under their packs and weapons, physically depleted: how could they ever clamber over that final pass?

That night they bivouacked near the Chinese forces. In his exhaustion, Jerry found himself thinking bitterly of what he and the other Niseis had done at Nhpum Ga. *We did it—and what did it buy the outfit?* They had been thanked by the brass; the men themselves had shown their appreciation. But the sacrifices of the 5307th as a whole had been unappreciatively absorbed back at Shingbwiyang as a big show of unusual stamina by a couple of battalions—and now let's get on with the war!

It remained to be seen whether the Marauders were able to get on with the war.

# CHAPTER 26

# The Last Mission

From the distances, the ranges of the Kumon Mountains looked velvety and alluring, but with nearness all the velvet wore off. In the warm drenching rains the Marauders crawled up the nearly vertical slopes of a trail which had not been used for ten years. The mules became almost impossible to manage as they slithered and fell on the steep hills. Then packs would have to be removed and the animals resaddled. Occasionally a mule would fall over a steep hillside and be killed. Each time this happened, equipment had to be abandoned, for the two-hundred-pound load could not entirely be redistributed among the remaining pack animals. Men discarded their equipment too—shovels and helmets, the stocks of Tommy guns—anything to lighten their loads.

At last the highest pass of all loomed before them—the Naura Hkyat, over a mile high, its peaks lost in cloud. At times men had to climb on hands and knees when the trail was too steep to stand on. Mules took the steepest pitches at a bounding run, some to make it, some to slide a hundred feet or more back down the trail, or to fall from it. In one day, a single battalion lost twenty mules.

They crossed the divide, staring at a bleak, dripping

landscape of mossy trees and rocks. It made Jerry remember that they were not so far from Tibet. They made a shivering bivouac, and started down the east side of the range. Two days later a new enemy attacked them, a fever which struck a man down like a bullet. A few men died; the others had to be carried on litters until a place was reached from which L-planes could fly them out.

The jolting descent ended at last. They were back in hilly jungle country, back in the rain, heat, and steam. Their maps showed that they were near the headwaters of the Irawaddy River. Of the force which had started over the Kumon Range, hundreds had been lost through disease and exhaustion. Dazed, the Marauders went into bivouac to take a supply drop from the air and study the situation ahead of them.

It looked, as always, simple enough on the map.

A rush southward across the Namkwi River . . . then a quick envelopment of the airfield at Myitkyina. But, in actuality, Mitch was fifty miles away, deep in enemy country. And taking an airfield near a big supply town might prove too much for a staggering outfit like the 5307th.

While depleted platoons were being patched up, scouts brought word that there was a garrison of 150 Japanese in the village of Ritpong, on the route to Myitkyina. Colonel Hunter, commanding the operation, realized that if they attacked Ritpong, the garrison at Myitkyina would immediately be alerted, dynamiting any hope of making a surprise attack on the airfield. But they were certain to be discovered by patrols from Ritpong when they attempted to pass the village. Hunter gave the order for Third Battalion and a battalion of Chinese soldiers to march on the village in an attempt to surprise it.

The attack was swift and completely successful: a hundred Japanese died in the initial assault. The rest were trapped by patrols near the village. But the Marauders' presence had been given away. All they could hope was that the garrison at Mitch might underestimate their strength and intention, and not prepare for a full defense of the airfield. Up and down the column the order went to step up the pace, as the force pushed on south. To Jerry, it was like a nightmare. How could anyone believe that this stumbling army of sick, emaciated veterans would have any striking force left after a forced march of fifty miles?

On the following morning, he was told to fall out beside the trail. There was a side trail here which ran out into the jungle. Several other reconnaissance men were waiting at the junction, including Russ. In a short time, Lieutenant Grissom appeared. He looked tired and stern. He had hurt his shoulder, and his arm was in a sling.

"I didn't tell you this before," he explained, "because they only told me this morning. You men are needed for a special mission. Any objections?"

The Marauders made no sign at all. They merely stood hunched forward to put the weight of their packs over their feet, and waited. . . .

"There'll be twenty other men on this mission, including a few from the weapons platoon. It was originally planned that there would be a hundred. But the way it looks now, we can't spare a hundred scarecrows from the line."

"What's the mission, Lieutenant?" one of the men asked.

"I'll let Lieutenant Cole explain it. He'll be in charge. All set?"

They nodded. Under their helmets their faces looked small and pinched.

"Lieutenant Cole is British, one of Wingate's men," Grissom added. "He was loaned to us for this operation. He's one of the best demolitions men in the business. He's been roaming around Burma with a few Kachins for over a year, blowing bridges here and there. He's waiting for you down the trail at the first *chaung*. Don't let his red beard scare you."

The *chaung*, a small river in a low, swampy area, was about a mile from the main trail. Here they found a group of men sitting on their packs. One of them was a big, red-bearded man wearing a beret. He rose as they approached, looking even larger. There was more meat on his bones than on the Marauders'. His beard was not truly red—it was a rich russet, like that of a fox. His skin was fair, with a few light freckles, and his eyes were a clear ice-blue.

"I don't know why Americans insist on fighting in the monsoon," he said whimsically, his voice rather high and clear, like the sound of a Halloween horn. "Fortunately, my fuses will burn wet as well as dry, so it doesn't matter too much to me."

They waited to be told what their mission was. Jerry looked at the other men in the little task force. There were two Kachin scouts, two heavy-machine-gun teams, two eighty-one-millimeter mortar teams, four BAR men, and some Tommy gunners. He thought with satisfaction that this was a record amount of firepower for twenty-odd men to pack. But the Army never wasted firepower, so it meant the mission was going to be a hair-raiser.

"Don't let me hear anyone calling me 'Lieutenant,'" Cole said. "It will only draw fire on me if we're in a brush with the enemy. I'm generally called Mad Mike, which will be adequate for this operation. Now, here's where we're going. . . ."

On the wet leaves he spread a topographical map. They huddled around it. Jerry could see *Myitkyina* ringed in pencil, as well as *Ritpong*. He followed the trail they were on until it ended at the airfield near Myitkyina. Mad Mike Cole drew the pencil from the airfield on an angle slanting southwest.

"This is Tambu Gorge," he said. "It is also a railway and a motor road. If you chaps had marched south from Nhpum Ga two weeks ago, rather than east, you'd eventually have come in on this road."

"If we'd marched south," one of the Marauders observed, "we'd be dead now. That's Jap country."

"Exactly," Mad Mike Cole agreed. "You'd have walked straight into Chenlun, the biggest Japanese garrison in the area. Which is what we're concerned with on this operation we're about to undertake. We've got to prevent the enemy from rushing reinforcements and supplies to Myitkyina from Chenlun after the attack starts. That would result either in our losing the battle outright, or in its bogging down into a three-months' campaign."

His pencil was moving again, following on down the Tambu Gorge until it reached a place ringed with pencil and marked: *Chenlun.* Between Chenlun and Myitkyina ran one of those slender, winding ladders which indicate a railroad. Mad Mike looked up with a bemused smile.

"Has any of you ever seen Tambu Gorge?"

They shook their heads.

"Well, I have. It's shocking country, really. The gorge must be a thousand feet deep, and in places the span is less than a quarter-mile! It was lunacy to try to build a railroad through that gorge, but it was the only way to get past the mountains, short of turning south a hundred and fifty miles. But the tea planters in the Shan states needed the road desperately, so the British government, who had taken over the country, had to undertake it. That was, oh, fifty years ago. You have something similar to Tambu Gorge in your own country—Royal Gorge, in Colorado."

Some of the men nodded, having seen it, and Jerry remembered pictures of Royal Gorge he had seen on calendars. It was a rocky pass, as narrow as a hall, down which a river brawled. On a vertical wall of the gorge, a railroad had somehow, by dint of dynamite and genius, been pasted.

Mad Mike was thoughtfully flipping something over and over on his hand. It was a blasting cap.

"Building that railroad was sheer virtuosity. Granite wasn't what gave them the trouble—it was earth-slides. When we had one of our heavier rains—say six or eight inches in a day—every yard of earth that wasn't pinned down by jungle growth began to slide. Everywhere they'd excavated, the earth would wash out. Finally the whole thing had to be shored up with teak logs. It's gorgeous—ten miles of reinforcing that looks like the wall of a log cabin. Dovetailed, cabled, spiked, strong as a fortress!"

"But vulnerable?" Russ remarked with a tired smile.

"Shockingly." The lieutenant smiled. "Of course when they built the railroad they couldn't know a chap like me would be coming along. You might say that I am to engineering what Genghis Khan was to China—ruinous. He was the first to use gunpowder, but I was one of the first to *mis*use it properly. I don't mean to sound boastful. I realize they've been using it to blow up bridges and the like for a century. But not with imagination. Bridges have been destroyed so clumsily that the enemy has simply set the span back on its moorings again within a week! Not when *I* blow them. When I blow them, they look as though they'd been held by pliers at either end and twisted. Of course," he conceded, "this isn't a bridge job. It's much simpler, in fact."

Listening to him, Jerry felt cheered and strengthened.

And that was the mark of a good leader, he decided—an ability to make it sound easy, inspiring men with the conviction that they were equal to the job.

"We're going to un-shore that roadbed," Mad Mike explained. "After we blow out those logs, the wet earth and rains will do the rest. Crikey! If we just pull out a few of them, the floods will peel the rest off a hundred yards a day! Of course the catch," he said, saddening, "is that the Japanese know that too. So they've fortified both ends of the gorge. At this end is a fortified island. The gorge is about a quarter-mile wide there, and the island splits the river."

He described in detail what they had to do.

They must march fifteen miles south today and bivouac near the gorge. Meanwhile the Marauders would be closing in on the airfield twenty miles east. In the morning Mad Mike's task force would start moving down a trail along the north side of the gorge. The railroad followed the south side, and because the river was at flood it would be impossible to cross to get at it.

"Except," he sighed, "at that fortified island. A native bridge connects the island with the north wall of the gorge. Another bridge connects the island with the railroad side. That's where we've got to cross, obviously. So the only problem is how to take the island. . . ."

Mad Mike frowned at the "fatboys"—the big eighty-one-millimeter mortars. His touring gaze included also the machine guns and other automatic weapons.

"There's a lot of damage in those," he said. "I only

hope the enemy isn't dug in so well that we can't hurt him. I wish we had a pack howitzer. But we can't fool around with mules or we'd lose the element of surprise. What we must try to do is to pin down the enemy while some of us go across on the bridge to the island. After we deal with the defenders, we'll go on to the railroad. . . ."

It was a different sort of war he was talking about.

It was hit-and-run, take-them-by-surprise warfare. Indian cunning and speed. That was Mad Mike Cole's specialty, Grissom had implied, but when Jerry thought of crossing one of those spidery vine bridges under fire he felt weak.

"Any questions?" asked Mad Mike.

"What if they cut the bridge loose when they see us?" asked one of the weapons men.

"They mustn't," said Mad Mike firmly. "We must lay down such a fire around its moorings that they can't get close enough to cut the vines that hold it. Anything else?"

Men began to rise and get under their packs. There was no use asking questions, because the whole project was one of belief in your good luck, and when you analyzed luck you lost faith in it.

"All right, we'll be off," Mad Mike announced. "The Kachin boys will show us the trail. A couple of you I & R men take the point."

Russ organized his group with Corporal Collins at the point, or leading. "We'll rotate every hour," he said.

CHAPTER 27

# The Gorge

The bivouac that night was in a flat teak forest deep with old leaves. The trees were just beginning to put out new green leaves. Since a fire was out of the question, there was no coffee. They ate their field rations, posted guards, and turned in. Before dawn they were moving about again, and as soon as the light was strong enough the Kachins led them southeast through the forest.

The forest ended and once more they were in jungle. A pack of baboons ran along through the treetops screaming at them. Mad Mike scowled. "Must be working for the Japanese," he said. "We couldn't give ourselves away better with bugles."

The country grew rougher, and once more they were wearily climbing the precipitous slope of a long ridge. It was not muddy, however, as they were the first over the trail in some time. One of the Kachin guides disappeared, returning in a few minutes to speak to Mad Mike.

"Prepare yourselves," the lieutenant said. "We're approaching the gorge."

The view burst upon them suddenly. They came onto a bluff tangled with vines and a few small trees. Below them they heard the roaring of water, like wind. The mountain range had been split open down a geological fault, and centuries of erosion had carved out a deep and winding gorge—the Tambu. Gazing east, they looked into it. Just below them lay the matted jungle, with the river, brown and frothy, flowing toward them, rushing toward the Irawaddy River at Myitkyina. They had to peer closely to discover the railroad on the far side of the river. A slender line of poles marked a telephone wire which followed it.

"We can't see the island from here," the lieutenant said, "but we'll be coming in view of it soon. We'll drop down to river-level presently. Remember we're almost certain to run into a patrol. I hope they haven't been apprised of our attack on Ritpong, but it's almost certain they have."

Again they were marching, now down a steep trail toward the river. At the bottom of the bluff was a larger trail paralleling the Tambu. As they entered the dark, misty gorge, they proceeded with great caution. A BAR man followed the lead scout. The weakening fear of what was around the next bend kept their heads turning left and right, while every now and then a man would glance up into the high branches for a sniper. This terrible fear, this trail-sickness, never grew less. It seemed to Jerry that the more you knew about combat, the greater was your fear of it. But your mind and body became a unit which acted automatically—until that point when the limit was reached. And no one seemed to know when it was going to be. A burly sergeant would suddenly begin to weep and shake, and though he cursed his weakness he was unable to master it.

This whole outfit, except for Mad Mike and the Kachins, had been carried long past the point where any man could be expected to continue. Lost in a world utterly strange to them, a world without roads, street lamps, houses, or civilians, a silent, green, steaming world of explosive violence, they had carried one another along by their mere presence—as if they were all a tiny morsel of their own world which held together somehow like a drop of oil on water. But now even that cohesiveness was beginning to weaken.

A guide came sliding in from the forest, raised his hand, and halted the column. Mad Mike pressed along to the head of the line. He spoke with the Kachin briefly. Then he summoned the others forward by an arm gesture.

"He says the island's about a half-mile ahead. But there's a trailblock a quarter-mile this side of it. Three men only, he thinks."

"A few shots probably wouldn't be heard over the roar of the river," Russ ventured.

"A few, perhaps. But they're almost certain to have a telephone or wireless. When we hit them, it's got to be fast."

He took off his beret and wiped his brow with his sleeve. Replacing it, he said brusquely, "All right, here's how we'll do it. We'll flank them on the steep side—there isn't room on the river side to flank them. I think a half-dozen gunners will be enough to dispatch them quickly. The rest of us will by-pass the trail while this is going on. We'll get into position farther along to lay it onto the island. As soon as we hear the firing we'll begin. We'll stay together, however, until we're near the trailblock."

For a hundred yards they stayed on the main trail. Then, with the Kachins using their long knives to hack away the growth, they hiked up the hill a short distance before turning west again on a line paralleling the main trail. The atmosphere was suffocating with moisture. The Kachins stopped and pointed down the hill. Mike Cole turned to Russ.

"He says the trailblock is just down there. Will you take two BAR men and a couple of Tommy gunners and do the honors? Give us about fifteen minutes to get into position—then hit them hard."

Russ led his detail down the hill after the Kachin. In a few yards they were out of sight in the jungle.

The main group went on for a quarter-mile. The lieutenant turned back down toward the river. Just then the faraway *chow-chowing* of a locomotive pulsed through the steamy air.

Mad Mike Cole grunted. "Not already!" he muttered. It hardly seemed possible that a relief train could be on the way to Mitch so soon. Since the river was not visible from here, he sent a guide up a tree to try to see whether the train was going to or from the airfield. In a few moments the guide was lost to sight in the branches. Very soon, however, he came back down the tree.

Cole listened to him, and sighed. "It's heading toward Chenlun! Thank heaven for that."

As they worked back down toward the river, the heat pressed in tighter. Jerry's vision swam. Cole halted the column suddenly and pointed downward through the undergrowth.

"There's the island!"

Between the clifflike walls of the gorge, like a submarine at anchor, lay a small island covered with low trees. There was little undergrowth, as though it had been hacked away for easier moving about. The island's shores were rocky. The river creamed around the passage.

From the bank, a suspension bridge made a long, sweeping dip to the island. The floor of it was the width of a half-dozen bamboo logs laced together with vines. There were bamboo side-rails, and the whole affair hung by drop-lines from two long vine-cables. From the far side of the island a similar bridge went on to the railroad. As they watched, three Japanese soldiers appeared on the bridge from the railroad, carrying sacks of supplies.

"Rice for his Imperial Majesty's troops," murmured Cole. "Just dropped from the train, no doubt. Look at those beautiful logs!"

His face had an ecstatic look. "Can't you see them beginning to roll into the water? And the whole roadbed sliding after them like an avalanche? Why, it would take years—! Well . . ." he took himself in hand abruptly.

"If you look closely you'll see a path on the island

near the bridge on this side. That's the path to one of the emplacements that guards the approach. There's another emplacement a little farther back, see it? Sergeant," he asked one of the mortar-men, "how many rounds would it take you to score on that emplacement?"

"I reckon I could bracket it in three rounds."

"I'll count on that. The other mortar will take out the second emplacement. Across the island there are other emplacements to guard the approaches from the railroad. Go after those as soon as you've neutralized the near ones. It's important—we don't want the clots running out and cutting loose the bridge shorings!"

Jerry watched the three soldiers walking across the far bridge to the island. Smoke from a fire fumed among the trees. Lowering his pack to the ground, the Britisher began laying out his explosives: fuse, plastic-wrapped high explosive, caps. The men crouched close to listen.

"Go on down and pick your spots," he said to the mortar-men. "I want you machine-gunners back from the bridge a decent distance, high enough above the island to lay it on anyone who shows his head. The Tommy gunners will be farther down—as close to the bridge as possible. The plan of action will be this—"

He sat back and peered down at the island as the mortar-men went down the hill.

"On my signal, the fatboys will open up and knock out the emplacements. That should shake up a little excitement. The gunners will go after anyone who shows himself. After we've done a little damage, the Tommy gunners and I will start for the island. We won't waste time shooting people we don't have to—just make for the far bridge. The gunners will take up positions at the approach to keep anyone from following."

Just then there was a tremendous rattle of automatic fire down the gorge. All of them straightened, startled. "Good Lord, what a racket!" exclaimed Mad Mike, alarmed. "The Japs have heard it, too—look at those men on the bridge!"

The men who were carrying supplies had just reached the island. Startled, they dropped the sacks and ran into the trees. "The fat's in the fire!" the lieutenant said grimly. "We'll just have to do the best we can. Let's go!"

Hurrying down the hill, they found a well-worn path which led to the main trail. Another sharp hammering of small-arms fire came from the trailblock. They passed the mortar-men, who were hastily setting up their weapons and laying out projectiles. "Fire at will!" Mad Mike ordered as they passed.

They reached the main trail. Suddenly a small figure came running along the trail from below. It was a Japanese soldier carrying a submachine gun. He wore a cap rather than a helmet, and Jerry saw, in that first shocked instant, that an officer's saber clattered at his heels. The Japanese saw them just then and clumsily brought his gun up, firing as he did so. A running trail of shots erupted along the ground from almost at his feet to a point just short of Mad Mike.

But now the Tommy gunners were firing, too, in a wild, deafening clatter of shots. The officer went down face-first and slowly rolled over on his back.

Up the hill a mortar uttered its flat, unresonant bark. A few seconds later there was a puff of white smoke on the island, about twenty feet beyond one of the emplacements. Then the other mortar hammered out a short, dry report and another smoke-shell exploded on the island near the second emplacement. Among the trees movement could be seen—soldiers were running to emplacements which had not been detected before.

The Marauders were late. With the sad knowledge of experience, Jerry knew that. The range was too great for them to drop any of those gunners before they reached their weapons. The Marauders were suddenly struggling down the hill to get set up, but they were late.

From an emplacement beside the bridge a string of smoke-jets trailed. Bullets began to cut the jungle growth. Cole struck Jerry's arm and pointed at the dead officer.

"Look him over! Get his gun. We'll have to blast away with everything we can lay hand to."

Jerry ran to search the dead man.

## CHAPTER 28

# The Island

In the officer's pockets were a couple of letters, a tiny bronze Buddha, a purse containing several pieces of Burmese occupation currency, and the inevitable diary. Jerry retained the diary and, as a souvenir, the Buddha. Souvenir! he thought. I must think I'm going to get out of this alive. There were three clips of extra ammunition in a belt-case, and he took these and the submachine gun and ran back to the others.

Near the river, Mad Mike was placing his men, while bullets clipped leaves among them. A small, folding pair of binoculars hung about his neck.

"The blighters! The blighters!" he muttered. He was disgusted and worried at having failed to surprise the enemy. For they had neither time nor ammunition for a siege. Undoubtedly other patrols were in the vicinity in addition to the one they had eliminated. They would be surrounded if they hung around the island too long. And by now the warning must have gone out over the island's radio that it was under attack.

Russ came jogging in with his patrol and they took

their places. From the island there was another blasting explosion of a mortar shell, followed by screams of wounded men. Through the dark-green foliage, Jerry peered across the river. A little man in a baggy uniform stumbled from one of the gun emplacements, his hands clutching his belly. There were two sharp bursts of BAR fire and he collapsed at the foot of the bridge.

"Good show!" Mad Mike grunted, peering through the binoculars. "Now for the other pillbox—"

The fire coming from the island was erratic. No mortar fire was being thrown at the mortar-men up the hill, though there must certainly have been mortars on the island. The firing seemed to be the sort which desperate men throw at a hidden enemy. Cole took up a position in the naked roots of a big, spreading tree, and Jerry huddled near him. The lieutenant did not fire his Tommy gun, but kept his glasses on the island and occasionally pointed out a machine-gun nest which no one had observed. Jerry fired the Japanese gun at a soldier in the trees, and Lieutenant Cole dropped his binoculars and glanced around at the small-caliber popping.

"Don't startle me like that!" he grimaced. "I thought there was a Japanese in our midst. As there will be soon enough, if we don't get on with the show—"

The mortars had scored on the second emplacement, but the gun was still being fired by a remaining gunner. "What did you find on our friend?" Cole muttered, resuming his search of the island.

"Letters from home, a diary—the usual stuff," Jerry said.

"What was his rank?"

"Major."

"Major! Well, well. That tells us two things: we've got their commanding officer, and there must be at least a hundred and fifty men based on the island! Probably two-thirds of them are scouting in the vicinity. He must have been inspecting the trailblock when he was killed."

"Sounds as though the attack has started on Myitkyina, then," Jerry commented.

"Why?"

"Well, a C.O. probably wouldn't be inspecting his defenses in person unless he was expecting an attack."

"That's true. Now we know why they're putting up such a puny defense, too. They're fighting without a leader. And they probably think there are three hundred of us, instead of two dozen."

The BAR's had taken out the remaining machine-gunner, while the mortars laid down an accurate fire on the machine-gun nests across the island. Suddenly a man sprang into view and ran onto the bridge with his hands raised. He was obviously trying to surrender. Cole was startled.

"What ails him? You don't suppose he's really trying to surrender!"

A gun chattered in the machine-gun nest the man had left. The soldier fell from the bridge, shot by one of his own men.

"That's out of character," Mike Cole complained. "They practically never surrender. I wonder how the morale is on that island," he pondered. "It must be low, or they'd be putting up a better show than this."

Suddenly Jerry thought of the diary in his pocket. He pulled it out. "I'll see what the C.O.'s been writing in his diary."

"Do that! If we could just convince them somehow that it would be a splendid thing for them to surrender—!"

Jerry turned the thin pages of the book, starting at the back of it in Japanese fashion, until he found the last entry. It was dated the day before. As he read, he heard Mike Cole shouting at the mortars to step up their fire.

"Patrol activity as usual," he read. "No evidence of enemy presence despite Ritpong attack. Men very apprehensive. I have again requested visit by medical officer. Four dead this week."

Jerry related what he had read. "Typhus!" exclaimed the lieutenant. "Possibly cholera. And no medical officer! No wonder they're edgy—probably all sick."

Jerry turned a page and read aloud a poem the major had written.

*"Like cherry blossoms in the spring,*
*Let us fall clean and radiant."*

Mad Mike grunted. "Let's fall right now, chaps—and let the nice demolitions squad get to work."

Hammering steadily, the mortars knocked out another emplacement. Then they began dropping shells in the trees.

There were cries from men hidden in foxholes. Tree-bursts were the most dreaded fire of all; there was no protection from shrapnel raining down from above.

One of the Kachins came trotting in from the trail. He spoke urgently to Cole, who turned and stared west down the gorge.

"The thing I greatly feared! The boy says there's a patrol coming a mile down the gorge. They've probably been contacted by radio. Bennett!" he summoned Russ. "Take five Tommy-gunners and set a trailblock. The Kachin will show you where."

Russ clambered up and named the men he wanted to follow him. Behind the Kachin, they started down the trail. Mad Mike struck his fist against a tree root in frustration.

"If this show doesn't get started, it will soon be all over for us! There's no help for it—we're going to have to charge the island," he announced.

Jerry stared at the thin, swaying strands of bamboo spanning the river. "I don't think we'd have a chance, sir. It would only take one gun to stop us."

"I know. But if we move down to the river, our own gunners can lay on a hot fire to cover us. . . ."

"If they knew where to lay it," Jerry protested. "We've knocked out all the emplacements we can see, but there are probably a dozen we haven't spotted."

"We've got to try it anyway," Cole insisted. "It'll be no worse for us than it'd be for those fellows at the airfield when trainloads of artillery and reinforcements started arriving. There's nothing else for it." He began collecting his demolition equipment.

"Wait," Jerry said thoughtfully, rubbing the cover of the diary. "I have again requested a visit by a medical officer," the major had written. So he must have been concerned about the condition of his men, and since he had written it only yesterday, the probability was that the men were at least as ill now as when he had made that entry. It was also probable that the troops had been stationed here for a year or more, that they were lonely as well as sick.

Here were two elements to work with—to mix like chemicals to see what new product might develop from them.

In his mind, the two words Major Morris had cautioned him against at Savage were flashing on and off like a neon sign: "*What if—?*" What if I went down there and pretended to be their C.O.—called on them from the bushes to surrender? (No—they would know it was not his voice.) But what if I put on his uniform? (No, because he was much smaller than I am.) Yes, but—*what if they really want to surrender?*

"Lieutenant," he blurted, "I've got an idea—"

"Good. I like a man with ideas."

"I'd like to try to talk them into surrendering."

His work-kit made up, the officer straightened up to stare at him. "What a delicious sense of humor!"

"I'm serious. I'll put on that dead major's uniform and give the orders in his name."

Staring at him, the lieutenant became very sober. "No, you couldn't possibly fool them," he decided gloomily. "Even from a distance, they'd know the voice was wrong."

"I'm not sure it would matter," Jerry reflected.

"You mystify me," the lieutenant said dryly. "Either you fool them or you don't fool them, Harada."

"It's a matter of psychology—Japanese psychology. A Japanese may be ready to quit, but he won't quit unless he can do it with good grace. If we give them an *excuse* to surrender, they may do it. An excuse may be all they need."

Cole sat back. "In other words, they may pretend to believe you're the major because it takes them off the hook? If they're *commanded* to surrender, they can do so without appearing cowardly, is that the idea?"

Jerry nodded.

Cole laid a hand on his shoulder. "You know, there's nothing cowardly about you Niseis, either. I haven't known many of you, but I can give your commanding officer an excellent report."

"I'd appreciate it, Lieutenant," Jerry said, thinking long, solemn thoughts that went clear back to Topaz, Utah, and a drugstore in Compton, California. "I suppose a good report is what most of us are looking for—as much as we want to help our country."

"A good report," Mad Mike smiled, "is what all of us are looking for, my boy. Get into that uniform, now. We'll try to make things uncomfortable for them while you change."

## CHAPTER 29

# Code of the Warrior

Much too small, the uniform constricted Jerry's shoulders and the trousers were too short. But it was otherwise roomy, and with the wrap-leggings snug about his legs it was not much worse a fit than the oversize fatigues he had been issued after the battle of Nhpum Ga. There was a smell of tobacco about it and, he thought uncomfortably, a smell of death. There had been four bullet wounds in the major's chest and abdomen, two in his legs. Yet there was relatively little blood on the uniform because he had died instantly.

Jerry cinched the saber about his waist and hurried back to the command post. Mad Mike stared at him. "Good Lord," he exclaimed, "you almost make me doubt your loyalty!"

"*Arigato, chu-i-san!* Thank you, Lieutenant."

Jerry saw that all the gunners had been sent down the hill and re-deployed near the approach to the bridge. Cole had strapped on his kit-bag of explosives and was ready to travel.

"I'm going down to the bridge with you," he announced. "It may carry more weight with the Japs if they know their commanding officer has already surrendered."

"I don't know, Mike—do you think it's worth the risk?"

"I think it is. I count on my beard to awe them." Mad Mike stroked his glistening chestnut beard sensuously. "Let's get cracking, Corporal."

They walked down the hill together, weaving through the dense tropical growth. When they reached the main trail, Jerry parted the bushes. He could see the smoke of mortar bursts drifting through the trees on the island, and puffs of cordite from a nest of rocks as a Nambu snapped spitefully at them. The clamor of their own weapons was deafening. The lieutenant gave the signal for them to cease fire. One by one the weapons went silent. The effect of this was to cause the defenders to taper off on their own firing, and then, puzzled, to quit altogether.

"I'll let them see me, first," Jerry said.

Cole squeezed his arm, and Jerry stepped out into the steaming sunlight. He raised both arms, facing the bridge. From the trees he saw a jet of smoke; an instant later a rifle bullet smacked into the tangled vines behind him. His muscles knotted with fear. He felt the blood pounding in his face. His body tried to turn to run back to cover. But he stayed where he was, hearing the lieutenant's voice behind him.

"Stand fast! He hadn't seen your uniform. . . ."

A trickle of sweat ran down Jerry's chest. He felt naked, spitted on his fear like a rabbit, paralyzed by the hypnotic eyes of all the weapons on the island. And looking down at himself while he waited, he had the illuminating revelation, *If things had been different—if I'd stayed in Japan after that year in Osaka—I'd have been wearing this uniform before now. . . .*

With a feeling of tears in his heart he thought of his parents—of Helen and Sam, and how proud they were of his being in the United States Army. I hope somebody's left to give them that good report, he thought.

No more firing came from the island. A questioning voice cried, "*Sho-sa! Sho-sa! Do nasai mashita ka?*"

Jerry walked forward, letting his arms drop. He halted a few paces from the bridge. Then he heard Mad Mike following him.

Immediately he called across the water, "Nothing is wrong except that we have been beaten, my soldiers. Nothing is wrong save that the war is over for us."

He did a Japanese about face and came to a smart salute. Mad Mike languidly returned the salute, and Jerry unclasped the sword-belt and handed him his saber. He stood with his head bowed while Cole possessed the saber and stepped back a pace. Then he stiffened again as though with resignation. He about-faced again and walked onto the bridge. Halfway over, he heard men calling to him questioningly, while one popped up from a foxhole cradling a Tommy gun in his arms.

Jerry halted and shouted over the growling of the river, "I have surrendered my command! There is nothing to be gained for the Emperor by fruitlessly losing our lives. Attention!" He saw the gunner snap to. "Place all your weapons in a pile by the bridge. Then line up."

He walked onto the island and stood there in his bloody uniform, waiting. The gunner came first, then a straggle of other men, several of them wounded. All of them looked terribly thin and sickly. The gunner wore a sergeant's insignia. Jerry spoke to him sharply.

"Sergeant, where are the other men? Bring them here."

The sergeant saluted and trotted into the trees. Jerry noticed that all the men stood with their eyes downcast, as though not wishing to look too closely at him. But all it would take to end the war for him, he realized, was one die-hard. One bullet from the trees, and the short, full life of Jerry Harada was over. He looked around, suddenly needing comfort, and to his relief saw Mad Mike leading a file of Marauders onto the bridge. He stood stiffly before the Japanese soldiers while the Americans reached the island and took security positions. The pile of weapons was growing—submachine guns, Nambus, a couple of mortars, a dozen Arisaka rifles.

The sergeant took his place before the prisoners and saluted. "These are all who are left, major," he said.

"Then it is finished," Jerry said. He turned and looked at Cole.

"Very good," the lieutenant said. "Stay with them. Throw the weapons in the river. I'll be back directly."

He left four men with Jerry, who ordered the Japanese

to lie down with their arms above their heads. Mad Mike Cole ran on to his chosen work.

Jerry had the radio and telephone equipment located and the radio destroyed.

When Russ brought his patrol back, Jerry said, "Want to get on the telephone, Lieutenant? There might be some news from Mitch."

Russ walked to the Japanese command post in the trees to monitor the telephone conversations.

Fifteen minutes later Mike Cole led the demolitions detail back, out of breath. Halting near the prisoners, he squatted down.

"Best to get down," he told the men. "There might be a bit of debris flying—"

At that instant there was a reflected flash from upriver, then a pulsation in the air, followed by a great, reverberating roar. Jerry saw huge teak logs blown from the bank fifty feet into the air. Mud, rocks, and logs ascended in a black geyser from the railroad embankment. A second explosion and a third followed. A section of embankment two hundred feet long was ripped away by the blasts, and now the rain-softened earth began to slide into the river. Rails and telephone wires disappeared into the brown flood. Vine-tangled earth crumbled away from the hillside, as a huge hole was opened where the embankment had been. The river clawed into it and brought more earth crashing down.

Jerry looked at the lieutenant's beaming face. He appeared to be hearing a symphony almost too beautiful to be borne. Blissfully he watched the earth-slide grow, spreading up and down the gorge from the site of the original damage. Suddenly he touched a drop of rain on his face and glanced into the sky.

"Do you know, I believe we're going to have a real downpour! Can't you just see that embankment after five or six inches of rain falls on it! Crikey!"

Russ came from the command post at his limping, storklike stride.

"What's the news?" the lieutenant asked him.

"I was getting something from Chenlun when the blast came," Russ said. "All I got was that a train had left for Mitch, per request of the commanding officer at the airfield. The blast broke the telephone line west of here, of course. Then Mitch came on and an officer said the field had fallen to the Americans and Chinese, and what should he do next? That's where it stands."

"It's perfectly plain what the blighter should do next," Mad Mike said. "He should get the devil out of Burma! The whole crew of them will be getting out of Burma now that Myitkyina's lost."

Jerry began peeling off the bloody uniform he had been wearing. He was terribly tired—more tired than he had been in all his life. The Englishman watched him thoughtfully.

"It's a curious thing," he said, "how a few small things can completely change a man. Given a different diet, a different education, and these prisoners here would have believed in the same things Jerry believes in. Seeing him in that uniform almost made you believe his mind would have to work the way theirs do, didn't it? But I daresay you saw the difference, in the way he bluffed that whole island down —to save our miserable hides. Seems to indicate that you can't judge a man by the slant of his eyes, doesn't it?"

Russ gave Jerry a wry smile. But Jerry was looking at the forlorn ranks of Japanese soldiers lying on the ground, defeated and humiliated. With their shaven heads and ill-fitting uniforms, they looked more like convicts than soldiers, and he knew from interrogating other Japanese that few had any knowledge of what they were supposed to be achieving by their sacrifices.

He told the Englishman thoughtfully, "Maybe when they get out of their uniforms they'll begin to think as we do. They used to, more or less—before the big brass sold them on *Bushido*—'the code of the warrior.' But they forgot to tell these warriors about typhus and mud."

There was a slash of lightning above the gorge, a bass-drum beat of thunder, and fat drops of rain began to fall.

"Destroy the telephone," Lieutenant Cole said quickly. "We'll be taking off now. Somebody tell the prisoners to stay here. We can't slaughter them, but I'll not be bothered taking them along."

He sent the Kachins ahead to scout the trail before they took it. Then, through the warm, heavy rain they started back up the gorge.

# EPILOGUE

Though the Marauders took Myitkyina airfield easily, it was only the first action of a long, debilitating campaign. Nearly three months after the capture of the airfield, the town and supply center two miles away at last fell to combined forces of American, British, and Chinese units. The promise to evacuate the Marauders after the taking of the airfield could not be kept because of a shortage of seasoned jungle-fighters, and many members of the 5307th fought through the entire campaign.

Yet the capture of the airfield by the 5307th was the first important crack in the steel wall the Japanese had built across Burma. With the coming of the dry season, their retreat from the land of pagodas, mud, and malaria was swift.

Merrill's Marauders were a small unit. They carried the lightest of weapons, ate the meagerest of rations, and were burdened with little credit even from their own rear-echelon headquarters. Yet they carried their own sort of heavy artillery—courage beyond the call of duty—and of the men who demonstrated this quality none were more outstandingly courageous than the fourteen members of the little group of Niseis who marched with them.

In his perceptive and beautifully literate history of the 5307th Composite Unit (Provisional), Charlton Ogburn, an ex-Marauder himself, says of them:

> All of us, I suppose, when we are moved to reflect upon what human beings are capable of, find that certain images come to mind as illustrations of surpassing achievement. One that will always leap to mine is a composite recollection of Nhpum Ga, and of no part of it more than the heroism, moral as well as physical, of those Nisei, Matsumoto, of 2nd Battalion, and in the 3rd, Edward Mitsukado and Grant J. Hirabayashi, decorated for—among other services—their persistent volunteering to go forward to intercept the commands of the enemy when the lead units were engaged by trailblocks.

And General Charles Willoughby, General MacArthur's Chief of Staff for Intelligence, states that the Niseis shortened the war in the Pacific by two years, in enabling the Allies to learn the real strength of the Japanese army.

But perhaps the real meaning of their sacrifices and courage for us other Americans is expressed in something General Joseph W. Stilwell—"Vinegar Joe"—had to say about the Japanese-American soldier at the conclusion of World War II.

> The Nisei bought an awfully big hunk of America with their blood. We cannot allow a single injury to be done them without defeating the purposes for which we fought.